Rainbow Fair

DIANA MA

CLARION BOOKS
An Imprint of HarperCollins *Publishers*

Clarion Books is an imprint of HarperCollins Publishers.

Rainbow Fair
Copyright © 2025 by Diana Ma
All rights reserved. Manufactured in Harrisonburg, VA,
United States of America.
No part of this book may be used or reproduced in any manner whatsoever without written permission except in the case of brief quotations embodied in critical articles and reviews. For information, address HarperCollins Children's Books, a division of HarperCollins Publishers, 195 Broadway, New York, NY 10007.
www.harpercollinschildrens.com

Library of Congress Cataloging-in-Publication Data
Names: Ma, Diana, author.
Title: Rainbow Fair / Diana Ma.
Description: First edition. | New York, NY : Clarion Books, an imprint of HarperCollins Publishers, 2025. | Audience term: Preteens | Audience: Ages 8–12. | Audience: Grades 4–6. | Summary: Twelve-year-old Chinese American Sophie learns about her Muslim identity for the school cultural fair while juggling expectations from her family and friends.
Identifiers: LCCN 2024012194 | ISBN 9780063339521 (hardcover)
Subjects: CYAC: Family life—Fiction. | Friendship—Fiction. | Muslims—Fiction. | Chinese Americans—Fiction. | Middle schools—Fiction. | Schools—Fiction.
Classification: LCC PZ7.1.M17 Rai 2025 | DDC [Fic]—dc23
LC record available at https://lccn.loc.gov/2024012194

Typography by Chris Kwon
25 26 27 28 29 LBC 5 4 3 2 1

First Edition

To my Muslim Storytellers family. This book would not have been possible without you.

One

I barely have time to catch a whiff of oily reconstituted potatoes and identify the smell as Tater Tots, not french fries, when Katie runs up to me, waving a sheet of paper in my face. "Sophie, you'll never believe what just happened." My best friend's face is shining with excitement. "We just hit a hundred signatures!"

My eyes go wide. A *hundred* signatures?!

Ever since last year's Rainbow Fair, Katie has been on a mission to fix the glaring lack of an LGBTQ+ booth. As she put it, if Monroe Middle School is going to appropriate the idea of a Rainbow Fair, the least they can do is include an LGBTQ+ booth. Technically, the full name is Rainbow Heritage and Cultural Awareness and Acceptance Fair: Celebrating the Diverse Colors of Our School, but everyone just calls it Rainbow Fair. Yeah, it's pretty cringey, but my amazing friend has been circulating a petition to get Principal Harvey to approve an LGBTQ+ booth for this year's fair.

I grin and high-five her. "That's great!" It's my signature right after hers at the top of her petition. Katie has been my best friend since kindergarten, so her fight is my fight.

As we walk toward the lunch line, I ask, "When are you going to give Principal Harvey the petition?"

"We're going to get assigned to booths soon." She gives a determined nod. "I'll give her the petition right after lunch."

"That's a good idea." A pang hits me. Does this mean that Katie (who came out as bi last year) won't be in the Chinese booth with me? I had kind of assumed that we'd be with mostly the same Chinese kids as last year. The other kids are fine, but I can't imagine running our booth without Katie. I mean, Rainbow Fair is bad enough, and my parents' enthusiastic support doesn't make it any better. No matter how many times I tell them that it's not a competition, they keep insisting that the Chinese booth will "win" again. So . . . no pressure.

But Katie doesn't need to hear how worried I am about doing a booth without her. She's celebrating a big win, and I need to focus on that and be happy for her. I grab an orange lunch tray from the stack. "I hope Principal Harvey approves the petition."

"Me too." She picks up a tray for herself. "Okay, my friend with the magic nose—what's for lunch?"

Katie always jokes about my nose. I can smell a ham sandwich all the way from the entrance of the cafeteria. Hot dogs and hamburgers are wrapped in foil and harder to smell, so I had to learn how to tell the difference between Tater Tots and french fries by smell. "Hamburgers and Tater Tots," I reply confidently. Hamburgers are always served with Tater Tots, and hot dogs with french fries.

It's a weird party trick, but even Katie doesn't know why I developed this skill.

Basically, if I have to trot out my usual excuse of "cultural reasons" for turning down ham sandwiches and hot dogs—I need to be prepared.

For one thing, I don't want Katie or any of the other kids to hear me mumble this super vague explanation to Ms. Krumm, who's in charge of the cafeteria line. Ms. Krumm is pretty nice, but she's forgetful. No matter how many times I turn down a pork lunch, she asks me for a reason. Every. Single. Time. I'm pretty sure it's in some standard operating lunch procedure handbook. I don't know why she won't just hand over the alternative lunch the school provides. I mean, it's not like there's a huge demand for the mushy apple slices, unsalted sunflower seeds, and vegan, gluten-free, nut-free, flavor-free crackers.

As we slide our trays down the metal counter, Katie glances

at me. "You're coming to my birthday party, right?"

Why is she even asking? We've been going to each other's birthday parties since we were five. "Um, duh. Of course I'm going to be there!"

"The thing is . . ." Katie avoids my eyes as she picks up a carton of milk. "It's going to be a sleepover."

My stomach sinks. Katie is Chinese like me, but her parents are the kind who say things like "Just try your best!" or "We trust you to make good choices."

My parents are different. They're the kind who say, "Make sure you reach your full potential!" or "Why would you need to sleep somewhere else when we've worked hard to provide a roof over your head, and anyway, it would be such a burden for your friend's family, and what kind of present could you bring to thank them for all that?"

In other words, my parents don't get the American concept of a sleepover.

"Will your parents let you stay over?" Katie asks, watching me closely. This is not the first time she's invited me for a sleepover, and she knows how my parents will react.

"I'll talk to them about it." Never mind that I have no idea what I'll say to my parents. All I know is that I can't let Katie down.

She squeals in delight. "Really? This is going to be amazing!"

But I'm barely listening to her. Panic is turning my bones into liquid, and my eyes are locked on the foil-wrapped object that Ms. Krumm is putting on my tray with a pair of tongs. Even though she plunks a white cardboard box filled with Tater Tots right next to it, the object in its shiny foil wrapper is too long and thin to be a hamburger.

It's a hot dog.

"But Tater Tots are always served with hamburgers!" I blurt out.

Katie blinks in surprise, and Ms. Krumm pauses in the act of placing a hot dog on Katie's tray.

Oops. I guess I said that out loud.

"There was a distribution problem with the fries." Ms. Krumm puts the hot dog and the Tater Tots on Katie's tray. "Don't you like Tater Tots, dear?"

As soggy and gross as the Tater Tots are, that's not the problem.

Katie answers before I can. "They're fine, Ms. Krumm." She turns to me. "Come on, Sophie. We have to hurry to get seats together."

She's right. Most of the kids have gotten their lunches, and the cafeteria is filling up. "Go on and get us seats," I say to Katie, my heart pounding. "I'll just be a minute."

She shrugs and picks up her tray. "Okay."

A tightness eases in my chest as Katie leaves, and once she's out of earshot, I push the hot dog and Tater Tots back to Ms. Krumm. "Can I get the alternative lunch? Cultural reasons."

If Katie overheard me, she would think I was lying about "cultural reasons" to get out of eating something that I don't like. But it's not a lie. For the thousandth time, I wish I could just tell my best friend why I don't eat pork. But after this long, it seems too late now.

Ms. Krumm sighs and takes my meal with her plastic-gloved hands. "All right, dear." She puts a new lunch on my tray. "Here you go."

"Thank you." I pick up my tray and turn to see Katie waving at me from a table in the middle of the cafeteria.

I imagine plunking my tray next to hers and saying, "Hey, you know how we've been best friends since we were five? Did I ever mention that I'm Muslim?"

Yeah, no. Katie will wonder why I never said anything before. To be fair, I never *meant* to keep being Muslim a secret, and it's not like my parents ever told me to stay quiet about it. But they also don't talk about it in public, so it feels all weird and complicated. I guess it was easier for me not to talk about being Muslim either.

I reach the table and squeeze into the space between Katie and Sarah, another seventh grader. Sarah scoots down to make room for me. She's Jewish and has the alternative lunch too. "Hi, Sophie."

"Hi, Sarah." I smile at her. Sarah has always been nice to me. I have a feeling it's because of the Great Pork Misunderstanding in kindergarten. I kind of blame my parents for that. If they had been just a little clearer about being Muslim, I might have been better prepared when the other kids asked me if I was Jewish like Sarah, who also didn't eat pork. My face heats up as I think of everyone at my cafeteria table staring at me as I stammered, "I don't think so . . . maybe?"

"Hey, Sophie, are you okay?" Katie waves a hand in front of my face.

"Yup!" I smile too brightly as I poke at a dry cracker. "Totally fine." After I came home from that day in kindergarten and asked my parents if I was Jewish, they laughed and set me straight. They also made sure to remind me that I'm Muslim every few months—not in a big, heavy way. It's more like "Let's have ice cream for dessert, and by the way, remember that you're Muslim." Or "It's time to go to bed. You're still Muslim."

So ever since then, I've been clear that I'm Muslim. But

I'm not sure what that means. It's kind of confusing when the only Muslims I see on TV don't look like me. I'm not Middle Eastern, don't speak Arabic, don't pray at a mosque, and don't wear a hijab, so how can I be Muslim? That's probably a lot of why I don't talk about being Muslim.

"Are you thinking about the birthday party?" Katie is looking at me with a worried scrunch on her face.

My face flushes. I had forgotten all about the sleepover problem, but now that I *am* thinking about it, I feel even worse. Why did I make it sound like I could talk my parents into letting me stay the night? "I'm sorry, Katie, but I don't think it's going to work. Maybe I can come for the party and just leave before the sleepover part." By "before the sleepover part," I mean before staying up way too late giggling and telling ghost stories in the dark while we're all snuggled up in our sleeping bags. Before the fun part. My heart twinges miserably.

"Do you think you could at least ask your parents?" She gives me a sideways glance. "You never know what they'll say. Remember roller derby?"

"They didn't just agree to roller derby all of a sudden. That took weeks of rock-solid research, divine inspiration, and a twenty-slide presentation." But yes, technically, roller derby is something that I talked my parents into.

"We could do a pajama party," she says, seemingly at random. "You could wear your new Wonder Woman pajamas."

Darn that Katie Yang. "Now you're just fighting dirty."

Her eyes light up as she goes for the kill. "Come on, Sophie! You have to convince your parents to let you come. We'll watch one of those Marvel movies you love so much to go along with your Wonder Woman pajamas."

I'm touched. That's a big concession for Katie, who couldn't care less about superheroes, as evidenced by the fact that she can't tell the difference between the DC and Marvel universes because Wonder Woman is obviously DC, not Marvel . . . and this is probably why I don't have many friends outside of Katie. At least I didn't correct her out loud. This time.

"But don't worry if your parents say no." Katie gives me a small smile. "Because it doesn't need to be a sleepover. It will be just as fun as a regular birthday party."

I can tell that she's just saying that to make me feel better, and I also know that she will cancel the sleepover if I can't be a part of it. *I won't be the reason for Katie's birthday plans going up in smoke.* "I'll convince my parents." I take a determined bite of the cracker that is somehow as hard as Wolverine's adamantium bones and weirdly crumbly at the same time. "You can count on it."

Two

I take a deep breath before I walk into the living room with my school laptop. Mom looks up from her own laptop, and Dad puts down his book.

"Do you need help with your homework?" Mom asks.

"Um, not exactly." Okay. I got this. It's not the first time I've had to do a slide presentation to convince my parents of something—like letting me try out for Seattle's tween roller derby with Katie. Not to brag, but my research into how hard it is for an Asian girl to get into a good college without a "brand" was inspired. Unfortunately, roller derby did not end up being my brand. But if I could convince my parents into letting me do a high-contact sport where I could easily lose a tooth or break a bone, then a sleepover should be easy. "I actually have a presentation I want to show you."

Dad smiles. "It's been a while since you've done one. Your recycling presentation was so interesting. Is this one on composting?"

Oh, right. I had planned to do a companion piece to the recycling presentation. "This is a little different." I open my laptop and begin to screencast my presentation onto the TV. It had taken longer than it should have to think of a good title. I had started with variations of "Why Sleepovers Are a Good Thing" or "Don't Ruin My Life" before deciding that I needed to ease into it.

The title of my presentation comes up on the screen in bright purple and pink.

SOPHIE AND KATIE: A FRIENDSHIP STORY

Dad's face falls. "So, not composting?"

"Okay . . . what's this *really* about?" Mom asks. She knows me a little too well.

"Just wait." I click to advance the slide to a picture of Katie helping me up the monkey bars when we were both six. The title of this one is "Friends Helping Friends." I clear my throat. "Remember how afraid I was of the monkey bars? Katie could have left me and gone to play with the other kids at the park, but instead, she stayed with me until I got over my fears."

"If this is about roller derby again, then the answer is no," Dad says. "We're lucky you escaped with all your limbs intact."

"It was just a few scrapes," I say, trying to stay dignified. I don't need to bring up that despite full padding and a helmet, I had managed to scrape my hands and legs, and get a huge bruise on my butt. "But no, this is definitely not roller derby." I click to the next slide.

It's a picture from a few years ago, and it's of Katie and me hugging, both of us bawling our eyes out. The title of this one is "The Tragedy of Separation (for the whole summer)."

"We're not sending you to horse camp, either," Mom says flatly.

I was actually secretly relieved that they didn't let me go to horse camp. I mean, I love the idea of horses, but I didn't realize how *tall* they were until I got up on a pony for the first time. "Totally agree." I click to the next slide.

It's labeled "Together in Everything." This one has a picture of Katie and me in front of the Fort Worden retreat center, where my Chinese school held its weeklong summer camp. Katie didn't even go to Chinese school, but she always came to camp with me because it was the only summer camp that my parents would let me go to.

Dad perks up. "Are you saying that you're thinking of going back to Chinese school?"

"Sorry, but no." Inwardly, I cringe. I should have anticipated that response. Rookie mistake to bring up Chinese school and raise false hopes. I went to Chinese school from third through fifth grade, but my parents finally let me quit at the start of sixth grade because I convinced them that I had too much homework as a middle school student to give up four hours every Saturday for Chinese school. Even then, they kept trying to get me to go back to Chinese school until last year's Rainbow Fair Chinese booth convinced them that I wasn't going to totally forget about my heritage. I almost remind them of the booth, but I can't lose the thread of my narrative by going down the Chinese school rabbit hole.

Quickly, I advance to the next slide, labeled "Katie's Dream." It has a picture of Katie and me in her bedroom with blankets around our shoulders, and each of us is clutching a pillow. We're looking into the camera with big grins on our faces. "Ever since I've known Katie, she's wanted to have a sleepover. Now she wants to do one for her birthday, but she says she won't have one if I can't be there for it."

Dad sighs. "I just don't see the point. Why can't you just go to the mall like you did for your birthday last year?"

For my twelfth birthday, my parents dropped off Katie and me at the mall for sushi, shopping, and the latest Marvel movie. "That was perfect for *me*," I say with absolute honesty, "but this is Katie's birthday."

"Sophie, you know we're not trying to be unreasonable. We just don't understand." Mom gestures to our bright faces on the screen. "It's obvious that you girls have plenty of fun together without imposing on Katie's parents to have you stay the night."

At last—an argument I'm prepared for. "That's a good point, and I wouldn't ask if Katie's parents weren't a hundred percent happy to host a sleepover."

"That's nice of the Yangs," Mom says, "but what kind of present would we even—"

I'm already clicking to the next slide. It's an image of a white box of chocolates with the distinctive Seattle's Sweets logo on it. "I checked with Katie, and this is her parents' favorite chocolate."

Dad squints at the screen. "Didn't Seattle's Sweets go out of business?"

"No," I say, "but most of their stores *did* close, and that's what makes this the perfect present to thank the Yangs for hosting me." I pause for dramatic effect before clicking to a slide with a link to a seasonal pop-up shop in a nearby suburb of Seattle. "This is the only place in the whole world to get this chocolate, and it happens to be open right now for only a month." I couldn't believe my luck when my last-minute research found this.

Mom's eyes light up, and I know I have her. "That would be a good gift." Mom *loves* finding the perfect present for someone. I kind of get that from her.

It's why I used my allowance money to bid on a signed copy of *Not Your Sidekick* (with a bookmark and a mug too) from C. B. Lee, Katie's favorite author of all time. I literally screamed out loud when I won the book in the auction. What makes it even better is that the auction benefited the We Need Diverse Books organization. The book is the perfect mix of my love of superheroes and Katie's love of queer young adult romance—bonus that the author and main character are Chinese. Katie is going to love it almost as much as she will love having a sleepover for her birthday.

Dad is looking thoughtful. I can tell he likes the idea of the chocolates, but for different reasons than Mom. He's super into the idea of kèqì, which is basically the Chinese way of out-politing each other. The way to get Dad on board is to convince him that my parents won't owe the Yangs a huge Chinese-polite debt for hosting me overnight. "I could pick up a box after work tomorrow," he says.

Yes. Excitement bubbles up in me. "Does that mean I can sleep over at Katie's for her birthday party?"

Mom purses her lips, but I can tell she's thinking about it

too. "How many kids are going to be at this party?"

"Five total with Katie and me." That makes it three more kids than have ever been at either of our birthday celebrations, which have always just been the two of us. But Katie made new friends since joining the LGBTQ+ Student Union. The club is open to allies, so I joined too, but I haven't gotten close to the other members the way Katie has. Maybe I'll get to know them better at her birthday party if my parents let me go. Of course they know Katie is bi and are fine with me joining the LGBTQ+ club, so that's not an issue. The problem is . . . there's a lot my parents just don't get about being an American teen. They're worried I'm going to care too much about American customs like sleepovers and forget I'm Chinese. That's never going to happen. I wish I could show them I can still be Chinese *and* go to a sleepover.

"Five girls is a lot for the Yangs to deal with," Mom says.

"It's really not." No one but my mom would think that five kids qualifies as an out-of-control rager. "And it's not five girls. Remember I told you that Katie's friend Shane is nonbinary and doesn't identify as a girl or a boy?"

"Oh, right." She has that carefully blank look on her face. The one she gets when her coworkers invite her to an eighties party or tell her to bring a casserole to a potluck—like she doesn't quite understand but is pretending she does.

But the look fades fast because I'm not her coworkers. I'm the one who put together a ruffled black skirt and fingerless lace gloves for an awesome eighties outfit and helped her bake that truly awful tuna casserole. "Is there anything we should do or say around Shane?" she asks.

"Or anything we shouldn't do or say?" Dad asks. He hasn't lost the expressionless look yet—the one *he* gets when his coworkers invite him to go for a drink. Unlike pork, alcohol is less of a hard "no" for my parents and more of a "drink in moderation" kind of thing, but I get the sense that his tech-bro coworkers aren't the moderate type. "We don't want to offend your friend."

That's the cool thing about my parents being immigrants. They know what it's like to be in a new world and aren't afraid to ask questions. Plus they get what it's like to be disrespected for a culture that others don't understand, and they're not about to do that to anyone else.

"Shane uses they/them pronouns," I say. "So you can make sure to use their correct pronouns."

"We can do that," Mom says.

"Got it," Dad adds. Pronouns are no big deal for my parents. They're already hyperaware of using the right pronoun in English because Chinese doesn't have gendered pronouns.

But I've gotten sidetracked. "So, if you think five kids is a lot for the Yangs to handle, then that's another reason I should go to the party," I say. "If I'm there, I can help Katie and her parents out."

My parents exchange a look, and I almost stop breathing from anticipation. They finish their silent communication at last, and Mom turns back to me. "You need to be polite to the Yangs and follow their rules."

Like I'd ever be rude! But they know that, so I just say, "I'll be respectful. I promise."

"Then I suppose you can go," she says.

My hands are so shaky with happiness that I can barely click over to the next slide, which says "THANK YOU" in big, colorful letters with animated confetti and balloons. I close the slideshow before I accidentally click over to the "just in case my parents say no" slide, which just has a big crying emoji.

Dad has an anxious crease on his forehead. "And remember that you're Muslim."

So they keep telling me. "Okay," I say, but confusing emotions tighten my chest.

Other than not eating pork, what does it mean that I'm Muslim?

Three

"I love it so much!" Katie squeals, flinging bright purple foil wrapping paper into the air and hugging the signed copy of *Not Your Sidekick* to her chest. She drops the book and scrambles over the floral rug in her bedroom to wrap me in a big hug. "Thank you so much, Sophie. It's the best present ever."

I smile triumphantly. I knew I'd rock that gift. "You're welcome."

The other kids at Katie's party exchange a look. I can tell that they don't get why a book is so special, but at least they're too nice to say anything out loud.

Allie says, "Open this one next, Katie!" If there's a leader in this group of friends, it would be her. People underestimate Allie because of her tiny frame, bouncy light brown curls, and sweet smile, but that girl makes things happen. "The three of us went in on a gift together."

Megan leans her cropped blond head on Allie's shoulder.

"I'm glad you remembered that we pitched in too." Megan always stands up to Allie's slightly bossy charm, but Allie seems to like that about her. It's probably why they make such a good couple.

"You're going to love this, Katie!" Shane chimes in, pushing their floppy brown hair away from their face. They're giving me a worried glance like maybe they get that it wasn't the best idea to leave me out of the joint present. "But Sophie's book is really cool too."

"Thanks." I smile at Shane because they're really the sweetest, but I don't feel bad that they all went in on a present without me. There's no way the three of them know my best friend well enough to get a gift as perfect as mine.

Allie hands Katie a glittery purple bag (her favorite color) with tissue paper in all colors of the rainbow.

Okay, I have to admit that the bag is awesome. It's possible that Allie, Megan, and Shane win in the presentation category. And it's also possible that I have inherited just a little bit of my parents' competitive spirit about things that aren't supposed to be a competition.

"Ooh," Katie says, digging through the layers of rainbow tissue. At last she pulls out a folded piece of clothing. It's purple. A flutter of unease goes through my body. So what if they know purple is her favorite color?

Then she shakes it out to reveal a purple shirt with the cutest darn unicorn (also purple) jumping over a rainbow with the word "PRIDE" printed underneath in rainbow colors.

Katie shrieks, "OMG, I love this!" Without hesitation, she puts on the shirt over her plain black top.

"It's a great shirt," I say, because it is, and the jealous green-eyed monster howling inside me can just shut up.

"Allie, Megan, and I all have one too," Shane says, their eyes shining.

Then in some kind of weird choreographed movement, they all unzip their hoodies to show off the same shirt as Katie's, except Shane's is red, Megan's is blue, and Allie's is green.

"Now we all have matching shirts!" Megan says.

Except for me, that is.

Suddenly, they're all hugging and laughing, and the jealous monster isn't just screaming anymore. It's throwing itself against my rib cage and digging its sharp claws into my heart.

Katie looks over at that moment. She lets go of the others and reaches over to pull me into the hug. "Sophie and I have matching shirts too."

My spirits lift as I hug her back. "That's right. From tween roller derby."

"Can I see your shirt?" Megan asks. A blush is creeping over her face, and she glances down at her own shirt like she's just now realizing that I've been left out.

Shane bites their lip. "Yeah, I'd like to see it too."

Katie gets up from the floor and goes to her dresser. "I've got it right here." With a flourish, she pulls out the yellow shirt with "Not Your Asian Sidekick" printed in red on the front.

Allie's face puckers. "Was that your team name?"

"Technically, no," I say, and exchange a grin with Katie.

Katie flips over the shirt to show them the "Rockin' and Rollin' Derby Girls" printed on the back. "That was technically our team name, but Sophie and I decided to add our own twist."

"Since we were the only Asians on the team." I don't explain that we had the words added to the front of our team shirts when we realized that we were spending more than our fair share of time on the bench. I mean, I get why *I* was benched, but Katie was actually good at roller derby.

It's too bad we never found out if our passive-aggressive T-shirt protest would have gotten Katie more play time or not.

Because I *literally* crashed and burned.

Technically, it was just the scrapes on my skin that burned. I didn't burst into actual flames, but I kind of wish I had because the crash part *was* both literal and memorable.

Our coach had finally put us both in the last scrimmage— Katie as the jammer and me as one of the three blockers. We didn't even get through one lap before I lost my balance and epically crashed with flailing arms, skidding skates, and everything. That would have been bad enough, but my path of carnage also took out Katie, all of our blockers, and half the blockers on the other team. Unfortunately, the other team's jammer escaped the wreckage and lapped us all so many times that they easily won the derby. Team dynamics were pretty tense after that, and when I decided to quit, Katie quit, too, in solidarity.

"That's so cool that you got to be on a tween roller derby team," Megan says.

"Yeah," Allie agrees. "I'm so jealous."

Before I can admit to how short-lived that experience was, Ms. Yang's voice calls out, "Who's hungry for pizza?"

We all jump to our feet and race down the stairs to the living room, where Ms. Yang has set out TV tray tables with plates, napkins, and juice boxes. There are two cardboard pizza boxes that she's just now opening up, and the smell of melted cheese . . . and pepperoni fills the room.

Luckily, one of the pizzas is a plain cheese pizza. Katie knows that's my favorite. She thinks I just don't like pepperoni or hot dogs or ham sandwiches and hasn't put together what all those things have in common. To be fair, I also don't like melons, butter pecan ice cream, salad dressing that's too vinegary, or mushy food—so maybe she just thinks I'm picky.

"Thanks, Mom!" Katie calls out as her mother smiles at us and leaves.

My mom would have hovered forever, asking questions to "get to know" our guests, but like I said, Katie's parents are different from mine.

I grab a slice of cheese pizza and settle on the couch next to Katie. Megan, Allie, and Shane squeeze in next to me with their own plates of pizza. I'm feeling so happy right now that I can afford to be generous. "Okay, Katie, since it's your birthday, I hereby release you from your promise to watch a Marvel movie at your party. Happy birthday."

Katie bows her head to me in mock formality. "I thank you for the reprieve."

Megan groans. "But I was actually looking forward to that. Don't let Katie off the hook!"

I look at her in surprise. I didn't know she was a fellow Marvel fan.

"Too late," Allie says quickly. "Sophie already said we don't have to watch a superhero movie."

Shane's eyes flicker between Allie and Megan. "I'm down with anything," they say. I can tell that they're used to being the peacemaker.

"I promise we'll watch whatever you want at your birthday party, Sophie." Katie puts her hand on her heart. "I make you my most solemn vow."

Megan whispers to me, "I can't wait to watch a Marvel movie with someone who appreciates them. Whenever I watch with Allie, she keeps interrupting to ask who's who and why are people turning into dust?"

Wait. Is Megan saying that she wants to come to my birthday party? Maybe this will be the first year I have a real birthday party with more guests than just Katie. I smile at her. "Yeah, Katie's the same way."

"What are you two whispering about?" Katie picks up a pillow from the couch and cocks it back like she's about to throw it at us. "Allie and Shane, I think they're making fun of us."

"No, no. We wouldn't dare." Megan blinks up innocently.

"Yeah." I widen my eyes and put aside my pizza. "We were just talking about how much we love explaining the Marvel Cinematic Universe to you all and would love to spend the next hour—"

Katie shrieks and reaches over with a gleam in her eyes that can only mean one thing: a tickle attack. But I'm ready for her and block her with a pillow. Megan, clearly no stranger to tickle danger, leaps off the couch and away from Allie. Shane, a big grin on their face, picks up a pillow too.

Soon we're all on our feet and running around the living room and screaming fake threats at each other. I'm laughing so hard that I can barely catch my breath.

Then, somehow, I'm clutching a pillow in my sweaty hand and facing the rest of them in their brightly colored matching T-shirts. My stomach sinks, and my laughter fades away. *I'm being silly.* It's not like the others have teamed up against me or anything.

It just sort of feels like I'm not even here.

Allie and Megan are locked in a tickle fight, and Katie is doubled over laughing and leaning on Shane for support as they cheer on Allie and Megan. The pillow drops from my fingers because I guess the pillow fight is over and I was the only one who didn't notice. I don't even know why it bothers me.

All I know is that I never felt left out when it was just Katie and me.

Four

Sunlight streaming into my eyes makes me blink sleepily and look around. *Where am I?* This isn't my bedroom, and I'm not in my bed. Thick cream carpet. Snuggly sleeping bag. Four other bodies sprawled across the living room floor in their own sleeping bags.

Excited realization jolts me fully awake, and a small gasp escapes me. I've just had my very first sleepover.

Next to me, Katie rolls over and opens her own eyes. "Zǎo," she murmurs.

"Zǎo." I whisper my good morning back to her so I don't disturb Megan and Allie on the other side of her or Shane, next to me. "Sorry. I didn't mean to wake you up."

"You didn't." Katie sits up and smiles. "I'm ready to get up anyway."

Megan groans from her sleeping bag. "I'm not." She pulls her pillow up over her head. "What time did we even go to sleep last night?"

"It's a sleepover," Shane says without even opening their eyes. "The whole point was to stay up as long as possible."

In that case, Katie's party was definitely a success. Firmly, I shove down memories of the tiny little weird moments and tell myself that I couldn't be happier that my best friend got the birthday of her dreams.

Allie bounces up from her sleeping bag and pulls away Megan's pillow. "Your morning grumpiness is adorable."

In response, Megan snuggles deeper into her sleeping bag. "Great. My girlfriend is a *morning* person."

Allie just laughs. "Good morning, everyone," she chirps, probably extra brightly for Megan's sake. Then she eyes Katie and me. "What was it that you said to each other just now?"

"Oh." I blush. "You mean, um, 'zǎo'?" Katie and I don't usually speak Chinese to each other when other people are around. It's not like we have a rule or have even discussed it. We just . . . don't.

"It means 'good morning' in Chinese, or just 'morning,' I guess, but the 'good' part is implied," Katie explains. She says it without a single stumble or tinge of redness on her face, and I'm in awe of how natural she seems to be with the other kids. But it's probably because she actually *is* comfortable with them, so maybe I should be too?

"Cool," Allie says, and that's that.

I let out a breath that I didn't even know I was holding. I'm such a dork. Of course Katie's new friends aren't going to think we're weird because we occasionally speak Chinese to each other.

"Come on." Katie unzips her sleeping bag. "We forgot to do the Korean face masks last night, but we have time before breakfast."

Megan shifts a bit under her pillow, and Shane opens their eyes. "A pre-breakfast face mask sounds great," they say.

I smile because face masks were my idea when we were planning the party together, and I thought Katie had forgotten, but now we're all getting up (even Megan) to go up to Katie's bedroom and stick wet, sweet-scented masks to our skin, and nothing in the world sounds better than that.

Ms. Yang walks into Katie's bedroom in a black velvet robe with pink silk lapels because that's just how she is. She doesn't blink at the five ghost faces that look back at her. "You kids look like you're having fun! When you're done, come have breakfast, but don't take too long. Your parents are supposed to pick you up in half an hour."

Knowing my parents, they won't just be on time but early. I

rush into the bathroom in the hallway, peel off the mask, and splash water on my face to get rid of the gooeyness.

With her mask still clinging to her face, Katie comes into the bathroom and hands me a towel.

"Thanks." I scrub my face clean.

"The directions say to leave it on for at least fifteen minutes, and we've only had it on for five," she points out.

"I know, but my mom is always early, and bad things happen when our mothers spend time together." I might be exaggerating, but no one can deny that things are always a bit awkward with our mothers.

It's not that they dislike each other. It's more that they're both Chinese and their daughters are best friends, so maybe they feel like they should be too, but they couldn't be more different. My mom is a superpractical accountant who always wears a variation of the same type of business casual dress in black, navy, or gray (with leggings and a sweater in cooler weather), but it's not like she's boring or anything. She just likes to be efficient, and she has a fun/mean streak of competitiveness that comes out during board games (I've never been able to win a game of Scrabble against her and probably never will). Ms. Yang, on the other hand, is a free-spirited art teacher who wears whimsical and colorful outfits that often have appliqués of flowers or birds, or both. Anyway, the pressure to be friends despite their differences has made for some strained interactions.

"Point taken," Katie says, shuddering. "I still haven't forgotten navel-gate."

I shudder, too, as I remember that time Mom came to pick me up from a playdate with Katie when we were eight. We weren't done with our Lego build, so our moms hung out while they waited for us to finish up.

And that was when Ms. Yang decided to show her navel piercing to my mother.

I have no idea how their conversation led to navel piercing show-and-tell in the foyer, and I don't want to know, but Katie and I caught the end of that scene. I'll never forget the look of embarrassment on Mom's face as she politely asked what kind of material the piercing was made of and the exact same embarrassment on Ms. Yang's face as she realized that she had miscalculated the effect of her latest friendship bid. It was almost as bad as the time Mom had given Ms. Yang a Picasso print from Ikea for her birthday. It's sweet that our mothers keep trying so hard to be friends, but honestly? It would be better if they just . . . didn't.

Katie touches the edges of her face mask. "I guess I should

take off my mask, too, so we can get down to breakfast."

I peer at my face in the mirror, hoping for the dewy flush promised by the mask's blend of green tea, pomegranate extract, and honey—but my skin looks exactly the same. Maybe I should have left it on longer at the risk of our parents having an unsupervised conversation. "I have regrets," I announce.

"Don't worry," she says. "I put face masks in the party favor bags. Make sure you get one before you go."

My eyes widen. "Did you just say 'party favor bag'?"

"I did," she says smugly, "and I'm not talking about the cheap plastic toys and random stickers of the party bags of our misspent youth either." She puts an arm around me. "I'm talking about *epic* party favor bags."

Again, I'm so glad my parents let me come so Katie didn't have to cancel her sleepover, ruining all this for her. "Not even one tacky plastic kazoo?" I ask, pretending to be disappointed.

"Not one," she says firmly.

"It's been ten minutes," Shane calls out. "Should we take off the face masks yet?"

I shrug. Who am I to deny everyone else their chance at supernatural glowing skin just because I panicked at the thought of leaving our mothers alone with each other? It's not like anything worse than navel-gate or Picasso-print-from-Ikea-gate can happen. "You should keep them on for the full time."

Katie grins and yells back, "Five more minutes."

Of course it takes longer than five minutes before everyone finishes with the masks and washes their faces off.

As we enter the kitchen, we're all laughing and touching each other's faces. Everyone claims my skin is just as smooth and radiant as everyone else's.

"Come and sit down," Mr. Yang says. "Breakfast will be ready soon." The table is already set, and there's a glittery silver gift bag tied with a purple velvet bow at each place setting.

"Ooh, they're so pretty!" Megan exclaims.

"Gorgeous," Allie agrees.

"Thanks, Katie," Shane says. "Best birthday party ever."

I'm so busy oohing over the party favor bags with the rest of them that it takes a while for me to register the unfamiliar smell wafting from the kitchen.

The doorbell rings, and Mr. Yang says, "Oh, that will be my sister. She's coming over to give Katie a birthday present. Be right back."

We all sit down, and my nose wrinkles as I sit next to Katie. Uneasily, I take a deep sniff and catch something oily and fried.

"Um, am I smelling pancakes?" Please let it be pancakes. Or hash browns. Or eggs. Or stir-fried eel intestines. Or anything except . . .

"It's bacon!" Ms. Yang says, turning from the stove with a swirl of her bird-appliquéd yellow apron. She's holding a pan, and before I can say "No thanks," she slides a crispy piece right onto the plate in front of me.

Of course, that's the moment when Mr. Yang comes back into the kitchen. With my mother.

I freeze, panic bubbling in my chest.

Mom's eyes lock on the bacon on my plate, and absolute horror spreads over her face.

"I wasn't going to eat it!" I blurt out. *Please don't make a fuss in front of all these cool kids I'm becoming friends with.* At least my mom won't make too big of a scene with Katie's parents here because of Chinese kèqì and—

Before I can finish the thought, my mother takes two giant strides to my side and whisks away the plate of bacon like it's poison. "We don't eat pork," she informs everyone in the iciest tone I've ever heard from her. "Cultural reasons."

Ms. Yang's jaw drops as she takes the plate of bacon Mom hands her. Everyone else is staring at us in shock too. Katie's eyes are wider than when I accidentally body-slammed her into the side of the rink at our one and only roller derby scrimmage.

My face flames up, and I just want to sink into the floor in utter humiliation.

But Mom is yanking me up out of my chair. "Come on, Sophie. It's time to go home." She pauses, and I can almost see the kèqì habits of politeness wrestling for ascendance. "Say thank you to Katie and her parents for hosting you." Oh, good. So my mother *hasn't* been kidnapped by aliens and replaced by a scary replicant after all. Which, on second thought, is too bad because that would have been easier to explain to Katie and the others.

"Thank you," I mumble, unable to meet anyone's eyes. This is shaping up to be *worse* than the kindergarten Great Pork Misunderstanding, and I didn't think that was possible.

"Uh . . . you're welcome?" Ms. Yang says, still holding a pan in one hand and my rejected plate in the other. I swear the bird appliqué on her apron droops.

Her hand like a steel clamp on my arm, Mom drags me away.

"Wait, Sophie," Katie calls out. "Your party favor bag!"

Mom doesn't even slow down, and I barely have time to snag my overnight bag from the hallway outside the kitchen. Twisting in Mom's grip, I turn around to face Katie and mumble, "I'll get it later." Assuming that she will *ever* want to hang out with me again.

The last glimpse I have is Mr. Yang gently taking the pan and plate from a frozen Ms. Yang, Allie, Megan, and Shane staring after us in confusion, and the beautiful gift bag at my empty seat.

And, of course, Katie—looking utterly abandoned despite her new friends and her special breakfast.

A pang shoots through my heart. It looks like I've managed to ruin my best friend's birthday after all.

Five

I wait for Mom to say something when we get into the car—either some variation of "This is what happens when we let you go to a sleepover against our better judgment" or "Oops, I totally overreacted about the bacon." Although, honestly, I'm only giving option B about a 10 percent chance.

But Mom just says, "I need to do some grocery shopping. Do you want to come with me or should I drop you off at home first?"

Oh right. Option C: pretend the totally awkward thing never happened. I should have known Mom would go for the classic response. "Drop me off, please."

When we get home, Mom doesn't leave to get groceries right away. She and Dad disappear into the bedroom, and I worry that they're getting ready to do a joint lecture. In my head, I form my counterarguments, which boil down to "I didn't do anything wrong!"

My parents come out of the bedroom, and Mom heads off

to do the grocery shopping while Dad asks, "Do you need any help with your homework?" He hasn't needed to help me with my homework for years, but he still always asks.

I guess I didn't need to mentally prepare for a lecture. "No, I'm good. Thanks."

"Okay. I've got some work to do, then." He pauses and says, "You should have some cereal or toast since you haven't had breakfast yet."

I guess that's as close as we're going to get to talking about the bacon incident. I should be relieved, but as I walk into the kitchen and open the cupboard to look over my cereal options, there's a heaviness in my chest. And it's not just the thought of having to explain all this to Katie at school on Monday. I keep thinking of my mother snatching that plate of bacon away and explaining that we don't eat pork for "cultural reasons."

Why didn't she just tell everyone that we're Muslim?

When I get to the mostly empty homeroom on Monday, Katie is already there, and a silver gift bag with a purple velvet bow is at my desk.

Okay, that's a good sign. "Hey," I say, like my mom didn't yank me out of Katie's birthday party with a super vague announcement about pork. I hadn't really known how I was going to play this, but I guess I'm copying my parents' strategy of pretending that nothing's wrong. "Thanks for bringing the party favor."

Katie isn't buying it. "What the heck happened?" she demands.

My heart sinks, and I sit down heavily at the desk next to hers. "Okay, so here's the thing. . . ." My words trail off when Megan comes into the classroom.

"Hi," she says to us.

We both say "Hi" back, but Katie doesn't even glance at Megan. She's staring at me like she's afraid if she blinks, I'll disappear.

Megan's face is full of curiosity, but she takes a seat in the next row, clearly deciding to give us privacy.

"My family is Muslim," I say in a rush. "We're not super religious. I mean, we don't eat pork, but we don't pray regularly or go to mosque. And that plastic Christmas tree we have every year doesn't mean that we're *not* Muslim." My parents had been very sure to emphasize that. "It's just that the tree was on sale, which is why it's missing half its plastic needles and is only three feet tall—"

"Wait," Katie interrupts. She barely seems to have been listening to my rambling explanation. "You're Chinese, so how can you be Muslim?"

Huh. That's her takeaway? I might be confused about how

I can be Muslim and not practice Islam, but I'm not confused about being Chinese Muslim. "That's . . . just who I am."

Katie's face scrunches up, and she doesn't seem to have a response.

The five-minute warning bell rings, saving us from the awkward silence.

"Thanks again for bringing me the party favor," I say, grabbing the glittery bag as an excuse to change the subject. "I wonder what's in here. Besides the face mask, which you already told me about."

As I untie the purple bow, Megan switches seats so she's right behind Katie. "I want to see you open your bag, Sophie."

I'm relieved that Megan's not asking questions about why my mom hustled me away from the party so abruptly. She probably figures she can get the scoop from Katie later. I wonder what Katie will tell her. My hands go clammy, and I have to wipe them on my jeans before I can finish untying the velvet bow. "Oh good!" I say, taking out the face mask. "A lavender face mask!" I'm trying to act normal, but I'm probably overdoing my enthusiasm, especially since I already knew about it.

"There's more," Katie says, doing a better job of sounding normal, though there's a tiny pucker in her forehead. "Keep going."

I take out another item. "Glitter gel pens!" I say, still too brightly. "I love these!" I keep going. "Lip gloss! So cool!" Argh. It's like I've never seen makeup before. "Essential oil roller! Also in lavender, which matches the face mask!" I can't seem to tone down my out-of-proportion reactions.

The smile on Katie's face is fixed, and Megan gives me an odd look.

I've got to take my excitement level down a notch. I clear my throat and take out the last item. "Cookies and Cream Pocky," I say like someone has just died, which is extra weird since it's my absolute favorite treat in the whole world, which Katie knows. Dang. I took that too far in the other direction. "I mean, these are super-duper awesome!" *Super-duper?* Who even says that? "I mean, they're nice." That wasn't right either. I'm like a weird emotional yo-yo.

"Um, yeah, I liked the Pocky too," Megan says.

"Thank you," I tell Katie, just wanting to end this conversation and put us out of our misery.

"You're welcome," she says, ultra formal like we don't even know each other.

"Good morning, class," Ms. Tucker, our homeroom teacher, announces, breaking into another awkward silence.

I scoop up all the cool party favors and put them back into the gift bag. *Okay, no need to panic, Sophie.* So what if there's a little weirdness between us? It won't last. Ms. Tucker is a big fan of partner work, so Katie and I will soon be writing a haiku together or analyzing a character in the book we're reading, and everything will be back to the way it was.

"Today, we're going to do something very special," Ms. Tucker announces with a big smile. "It's time to sign up for Rainbow Fair!"

Six

"I am so honored to be the chair of the steering committee for the Rainbow Heritage and Cultural Awareness and Acceptance Fair," Ms. Tucker says, and then has to take a breath before she can get the rest of the title out. "Celebrating the Diverse Colors of Our School." Another breath. "I'm sure that this year's fair will be wonderful." Ms. Tucker chaired the steering committee last year too, and from the way she talks about Rainbow Fair, it's clear she's super invested. The glazed eyes and slumped bodies of most of her students don't seem to faze her.

Katie gives me a quick glance and whispers, "Sophie, I meant to tell you—"

"You haven't told her yet?" Megan asks, interrupting Katie.

Wait. Megan knows something that I don't?

"No talking, girls." The pleasant expression on Ms. Tucker's face never wavers.

"Sorry," Katie mumbles.

I wonder what it was that she wanted to tell me. If things hadn't been so awkward after the bacon incident, I'm sure I'd know already.

"You've all submitted your cultural surveys," Ms. Tucker says, "and I have your Rainbow Fair booth assignments right here." With a big flourish, she picks up a multicolored folder from her desk. Now she'll read each student's name and the booth we've been assigned, not that there's any mystery about it. I'll be in the Chinese booth with Katie and Henry, both seventh graders like me. Last year's seventh graders are eighth graders now, who are allowed to opt out of Rainbow Fair, but that's okay. I'm sure we'll pick up a couple of Chinese sixth graders. I already know one of them—a girl named Rowan. Come to think of it, the four of us might be it. It's not like our mostly white middle school has a lot of Chinese kids.

Ms. Tucker starts reading names in alphabetical order and booth assignments, and everyone looks bored. Unlike the Sorting Hat ceremony in *Harry Potter*, we all know where we're going to end up.

Ms. Tucker assigns Tyler Greene to the Irish booth and then says, "Sophie Hu, Chinese booth." Like I said, no surprise there. "And, Katie, you'll be with Sophie, I'm sure," she says, even though she's nowhere near the end of the list, where Katie's last name, Yang, puts her.

Katie's hand shoots into the air.

Ms. Tucker's eyebrows lift up. "Yes, Katie?"

"Did Principal Harvey tell you about the new booth?"

New booth? My heart does a somersault like it's jumping for joy and sinking in disappointment all at the same time. This can mean only one thing.

"The LGBTQ+ booth has just been approved, and I'm going to be in that booth." Katie glances at me.

I beam at her. "That's awesome," I whisper, determined to project nothing but support and positive vibes.

Even though the Chinese booth won't be any fun without her.

As Ms. Tucker moves her finger down her list to check, Katie whispers back, "Sorry I didn't get to tell you before."

Ms. Tucker looks up and smiles. "Ah, yes. Here it is. You've been assigned to the new LGBTQ+ booth, Katie. And you too, Megan." Megan's last name, James, puts her right after me.

I smile so hard at them both that my face feels all stretched out. "It's really great news." I mean it too. I just wish there were a way Katie could still be in the Chinese booth with me.

Ms. Tucker continues down the list until everyone in the class has been assigned to their booths. Me in the Chinese culture booth, Katie and Megan in the new LGBTQ+ booth, a kid named Lucas in the Black culture booth, Sarah in the

Jewish culture booth, and the rest of the kids split among the other categories on the cultural survey. I'm still not sure if a single question that asks you to pick the culture that you "most identify with" qualifies as a survey.

"You can go to your school portal to find out who else is in your booth," Ms. Tucker says, clearly expecting that we're all going to scramble for our school-issued laptops to check out our booth teams.

No one moves.

She frowns. "Class, open your laptops and check your booth assignments." That's how we can tell she's really excited about the whole Rainbow Fair thing. Ms. Tucker is totally old-school and never has us use our laptops for anything. There's a lot of shuffling and noise as we take our laptops from the depths of our individual backpacks.

I go into my school portal and click on the animated dancing rainbow icon marked Rainbow Fair (in rainbow colors, of course). Katie is so right that the school has appropriated gay culture and that it's beyond time for an LGBTQ+ booth.

There's a list of about a dozen cultures, and I click on "Chinese." It goes immediately to a page with three names. Me, Henry, and Rowan. I sigh and think about my parents' expectation that the Chinese booth will "win" again this year. Well, there won't be any winning, imaginary or not, with just the three of us and without Katie's creativity. On the bright side, maybe our sure-to-be-subpar booth will finally convince my parents that Rainbow Fair isn't a competition.

"Who else is in the Chinese booth?" Katie asks.

"Henry and Rowan." Neither of them are in our homeroom. "It should be fun," I say, determined to pretend that everything is fine.

"I'll give you some time in class to brainstorm with the other students in your booth." Ms. Tucker pauses as her gaze lands on me. "Sophie, Sarah, and Lucas, since none of your other boothmates are in this class, you can work together for now."

The three of us exchange a look, and Lucas somehow manages to smile and roll his eyes at the same time like he's saying, "This is pathetic, but I'm not holding it against you." Or at least I hope that's what his eye-roll-and-smile combo meant.

Sarah raises her hand. "It looks like each group has an online discussion board. Can we spend our group time posting in the discussion?"

I sneak a look at my screen. She's right. There is a link to a discussion board at the bottom of the list of names.

"I suppose that would be fine, but after you post, make sure you share something about your culture with your group members," Ms. Tucker says. "Now, go find your groups."

I pack my stuff to move, but I'm distracted by Katie and Megan putting their desks together. "Let's out-rainbow everyone else!" Katie says. Her competitive spirit is exactly why the Chinese booth was number one last year. *Darn it—not a competition!* It's not like the booths are scored or there are any prizes. My parents are clearly getting inside my head.

Sarah and Lucas both come over to me, and we exchange awkward hellos before turning our attention to our individual laptops. All the other groups are talking to each other too, but none of us sound as enthusiastic as Katie and Megan. Then again, no one else has a reason to be excited about Rainbow Fair.

With a sigh, I click on the link to the Chinese booth discussion. Rowan and Henry have already posted.

> **Rowan: So excited for my first Rainbow Fair!!!**

Okay, I stand corrected. Rowan apparently has a reason to be excited about Rainbow Fair, but that's kind of just how she is.

> **Henry: Welcome Rowan!**
> **Rowan: Thanks Henry!** 🌈💖😄

I type my own welcome to Rowan, and she responds with even more emojis.

> Henry: Sophie, why isn't Katie in our booth?
> Rowan: Yeah, I didn't see Katie's name. It's a mistake, right? 🥺
> Henry: Seriously, Sophie, what's going on?

My stomach twists. I'm not looking forward to telling them that our little booth is down to three kids. At least the Chinese booth isn't the only small booth. Last year, the Korean, Japanese, and Pacific Islander booths all had about the same number of kids as we did. The Southeast Asian, South Asian, and Central Asian booths might have been bigger, but not by much. But this is not about me.

"What about posters of gay pop culture icons?" Megan is asking.

"Love it!" The joy practically vibrates through Katie's voice.

I start typing. **Katie got the LGBTQ+ booth approved and is going to be in that booth. So happy for her!**

> Rowan: Good for her! 💗💗💗
> Henry: What?! Katie is the reason our booth was so good last year.

He's not wrong, but I'm a little offended. I mean, I wasn't the one who did calligraphy of ancient Tang dynasty poems or made paper lanterns to decorate our booth, but that doesn't mean I *can't* do those things. **I'm still in the Chinese booth. It will be fine.**

Henry: Okay.

Rowan: I'm sure it will be great!!!

I'm not sure which worries me more—Henry's underwhelmed reaction or Rowan's enthusiastic vote of confidence.

Seven

Ms. Tucker wanders over as I'm finishing up the online discussion with Rowan and Henry. "Don't spend all your time online," she says to Lucas, Sarah, and me. "You should be sharing with each other too."

Lucas looks up from his laptop. "Our booth is going to be a display of books by Black authors like Jason Reynolds, Dhonielle Clayton, and Renée Watson."

"That's awesome!" I say.

"Yeah, very cool," Sarah says.

I wait for Katie to jump in, but I forgot that she's not in my group. She's talking with Megan and can't hear our conversation.

Lucas grins at us. "Thanks. The Black Student Union has been reading and talking about books by Black authors, and we thought it would be good to share them."

"That's nice, but shouldn't you also have something more . . ." Ms. Tucker clears her throat. "Maybe your booth could include more cultural things from Africa?"

Oh no. My breath whooshes out, and I literally cringe.

I know I should say something, but my tongue feels thick and I don't know what. Katie would have known exactly what to do, but I'm not Katie.

Lucas's face closes off. "Why?"

"Because..." Ms. Tucker's voice trails off as he just watches her without speaking. "Never mind." She laughs nervously. "I'm sure your booth will be just fine."

She turns to me. "And what will the Chinese booth be doing this year? I still remember the model of a pagoda from last year." I could swear her eyes are getting misty from the memory.

Yeah, the pagoda was all Katie. I can't tell Ms. Tucker that I just spent the last fifteen minutes reassuring Henry and Rowan that our booth won't be ruined just because Katie's not in our group this year. "Um, we haven't quite figured out the details yet."

"Well, you're just getting started. I'm sure it will be wonderful." Then Ms. Tucker looks at Sarah. "What's the Jewish cultural booth doing this year?"

"Um, food and stuff?" Sarah mumbles. "Probably the same thing as last year."

"Perfect!" Ms. Tucker beams.

Huh? How is it that our vague answers about the Chinese and Jewish booths are somehow more acceptable than the cool, unique idea that the Black Student Union came up with?

"I'm so glad that we have a Jewish booth," Ms. Tucker continues. "It's too bad that we don't have a Muslim booth too. We did have one a couple of years ago, but the kid who ran it is in high school now. Sadly, no one else has stepped up." She sighs. "If only we had a student who could represent the beautiful Islamic culture . . ."

I squirm in my chair and don't look at Katie.

Sarah and Lucas are looking down at their desks and seem uncomfortable too, so maybe my sweaty palms and hot face don't seem too weird.

Ms. Tucker drifts back to the front of the room. "Five more minutes to wrap up your conversations, class."

Sarah and Lucas go back to their laptops, and everyone else keeps talking to each other.

That's when Katie scoots her chair over to me, so intent on me that she doesn't seem to notice that one of those weirdly random pockets of silence has just fallen over the room.

Stomach cramping, I open my mouth to interrupt her, but it's like I'm in one of those slow-motion nightmares where I'm powerless to stop what's about to happen.

"So *are* you Muslim?" she whispers a little too loudly. The whole class swivels over to us, and Katie claps her hand over her mouth as she realizes what she's done.

My face goes fiery hot, and before I can respond, Ms. Tucker rushes over to me, her eyes lighting up. "Sophie, you're Muslim?"

Katie, looking horrified, mouths "Sorry" at me, and it's not her fault, but everyone in the class is staring at me, and it feels like there are a hundred bees in my stomach.

"Uh," I stammer. My heart is pounding so hard that I'm sure it's going to burst right through my chest. "Yes?"

It's not exactly a confident answer, but Ms. Tucker leaps on my revelation with joy. "Wonderful! You can run a Muslim booth."

What the actual heck?! "Wait!" I blurt out. "My family doesn't practice, and I don't really know much about Islam."

"That doesn't matter!" She makes a little waving motion. "It will be such an amazing opportunity for you to discover your culture." *Oh no.* Ms. Tucker thinks my protests are just false modesty. "Why, I learned so much about my own heritage when I helped out with the Irish booth last year."

I have no idea how to explain that helping out with the Irish booth and being the only Muslim kid in the school running the Islamic cultural booth are two totally different things.

But . . . would it actually be so awful to find out about being

Muslim? I'm not thrilled about Katie accidentally revealing that I'm Muslim, but now that it's out there, maybe I should just go all in. My parents are always talking about how "all or nothing" I am.

My parents! My mouth goes dry. I'm not sure how they'll feel about me running a Muslim booth—on one hand, the constant reminders that I'm Muslim, and on the other hand, the excuse of "cultural reasons" for not eating pork instead of just telling people we're Muslim. But I'm crystal clear on how they feel about the Chinese booth. They definitely wouldn't want me to quit that. "Um, would I have to give up the Chinese booth to run another booth?"

"Well, we generally have students participate in just one booth." A little pucker of worry forms on Ms. Tucker's forehead, so maybe it's registering that I'm not exactly reacting with glee to her suggestion that I run a Muslim booth. "Of course it's fine if you'd like to stay with the Chinese booth."

She's offering me an out. I should take it, but my throat tightens, and I can't seem to say that I want to stay in the Chinese booth. Because maybe I don't. I glance at Katie, who's mouthing, "You don't have to do this."

But she's doing something different, so why shouldn't I? I don't want to do the same old Chinese booth without my best friend. Besides, looking into Islam can't be any worse than putting all that work into researching roller derby only to crash and burn. *Okay, fine.* Some part of me wants to figure out what it means for me to be Muslim. "No, that's all right," I mutter at last.

I hear Katie's sharp intake of breath, but an iron core of determination is forming in me. If my best friend is exploring a new aspect of her identity, then so can I. *All or nothing.* Right. "You can put me in the Muslim booth."

Delight rushes back into Ms. Tucker's face. "Excellent. I'll inform the Rainbow Fair Committee and make the change."

It looks like I'm running the Muslim booth.

Eight

Katie grabs my arm right after class ends and pulls me outside Ms. Tucker's room. "Your parents are going to kill you for giving up the Chinese booth."

"I know! What was I thinking?" I still want to do the Muslim booth, but it's sinking in just how disappointed my parents are going to be about the Chinese booth. I mean, doing the Chinese booth last year was the only thing that slowed down their campaign to get me back into Saturday Chinese school. Am I going to have to give up four hours every Saturday morning just to convince my parents I still have Chinese pride? I clutch Katie as a wave of students carry us down the hallway. "You've got to help me."

"It's okay," she says. "Just tell Ms. Tucker you've changed your mind and want to be put back into the Chinese booth."

"No, no." That's not what I meant. "I'm going to stick with the Muslim booth, and I need your help in keeping my parents from finding out that I'm not doing the Chinese booth."

Her eyes widen and she stops right in the middle of the hall. A kid almost runs into her, and I pull her aside into a spot between two banks of lockers. "You're going to help me, right?" I ask.

Katie hesitates for a second. "Are you sure you want to lie to your parents? I mean . . . that's not really your style." Maybe she's thinking of how I told my parents all about my roller derby disaster even though she had specifically warned me not to. Katie had been afraid it would make them reluctant to let me do any other extracurricular activity, and she was right.

"It's not exactly lying," I hedge. "I'm just leaving out the fact that I'm dropping the Chinese booth."

"What's going to happen when they ask you how the Chinese booth is going?" She narrows her eyes at me. "I know how you are. You're going to crack."

I lean my head against the cold metal side of a locker. "You're right," I wail. "What am I going to do?"

Katie pulls me off my locker pillow and puts both hands on my shoulders. "Relax, Sophie. I'm going to get you through this."

"Really?" I ask hopefully. "How?"

She takes her hands off my shoulders and puts them on her hips instead. "For starters, I'm going to pretend to be your mother, and we're going to practice ly—I mean, keeping the truth from her."

"That's not how my mother stands."

She rolls her eyes and takes her hands off her hips. "Just go with it."

I'm not sure that this role-play is going to help, but it doesn't really matter. What does matter is that Katie is on my side, and that makes me feel I can do anything. "Okay, Mom."

"My darling little Sophie, did you have an amazing time at school today?"

"Have you even *met* my mother?"

"Sorry, I couldn't help it," she says with a grin. "For real this time." She clears her throat. "Sophie, how was school?" She still doesn't sound like my mom, but at least it's something my mom would say.

"It was fine." So far so good. Maybe keeping the truth from my parents won't be so hard after all. . . .

"Who's with you in the Chinese booth this year?"

Instantly, my face turns hot, and sweat prickles at my scalp. "Um, what Chinese booth?" I squeak, utterly panicked.

"Seriously? One question is all it takes to break you?"

I sigh and eye the hallway that's emptying out of everyone but the stragglers and us. "We'd better get to class, but maybe we can practice more later."

"All right." Katie takes a step in the direction of her class but then pauses. "Sophie?"

"Yeah?" I don't want to be late to my science class, but Katie is shifting from foot to foot like she has something important on her mind but doesn't quite know how to say it.

"I'm sorry I outed you," she mumbles.

I just gape at her because I have no idea what she's talking about.

"I didn't mean for anyone to hear when I asked if you were Muslim."

It's weird, but I had forgotten how everyone in my homeroom found out I was Muslim. And I wasn't trying to hide being Muslim. It was just something I didn't talk about. "Oh, that. It's okay." And it is, actually. Katie didn't mean to tell everyone, and it kind of feels . . . "nice" isn't the right word, *but* fine that people know I'm Muslim. Maybe that's why I want to do the Muslim booth.

"So you *are* Muslim?"

"Yes." My chest tightens, but I need to say it. "I'm Muslim." My heart full-on stops and then comes back to life in slow, sluggish beats. It's the first time I've said those words out loud.

Katie seems to be waiting for more, but I don't know what else there is.

"So about that," she finally says. "Why didn't you tell me,

your best friend, that you're Muslim?"

Fair question. But my stomach tightens because I don't know how to answer her. *I don't even know what it means for me to be Muslim. How was I supposed to explain it to Katie?*

The shrill ring of the late bell blasts from the intercom, making me jump. "Ack! We're late!"

Katie doesn't move.

"Listen," I say quickly, backing away in the direction of science class. "Let's talk at lunch, but I swear I wasn't trying to keep a secret from you or anything like that." *I was just too confused by what it means to be Muslim to talk to you about it.* I don't say the words out loud.

Instead, I turn and run to class before she can answer, and maybe I don't want to hear her response—which would be a first.

My stomach cramps, and it's not because I'm flying down the hallway with my backpack flapping up and down and smacking my waist or the fact that I'm late to class.

How can I not want to know what my best friend has to say?

As I sit down at the cafeteria table with my alternative lunch, the intercom crackles, and Principal Harvey's voice booms out. "Happy Monday, Monroe Middle School students! I am pleased to announce that this year's Rainbow Fair will include two new booths! An LGBTQ+ booth and a Muslim booth."

My stomach falls. What is Katie going to think of the LGBTQ+ booth being announced at the same time as the Muslim booth? She had to get over a hundred signatures for her booth while I literally did nothing to get my new booth.

"If you want to switch from your current choice of booths to one of the new ones, please see Ms. Tucker, lead faculty advisor of the Rainbow Fair Committee," Principal Harvey continues. "All changes must be requested by the end of school on Friday. Let's make this Rainbow Fair the best yet!"

I don't know if it will be the best one yet, but it will be *something*.

Katie plunks her lunch tray next to mine on the table, but instead of commenting on Principal Harvey's announcement, she looks pointedly at the flavor-free lunch option on my tray and then to the ham sandwich on her own tray. "Is *that* why you don't eat hot dogs and ham sandwiches and pepperoni pizza?" She doesn't clarify what she means by "that," but I get it.

"Yes." I put down my package of unsalted sunflower seeds and take a breath. "I don't eat pork because I'm Muslim." My heart skips as I speak, but at least it doesn't feel like my heart is going to give out like it did before. Maybe it will get easier each time I say I'm Muslim.

I wait for Katie to ask me again why I had kept it a secret from her. I still don't know how to answer that question.

Instead, Katie picks up one of my dry crackers and takes a bite. She makes a face and sets it down. "Then we're going to have to get you a better alternative lunch. I'm thinking of a petition."

Of course she is. I'm grinning so big that my face kind of hurts. "That sounds like a good idea."

She nods but adds, "That just leaves one problem. Your parents are still expecting you to do the Chinese booth, right?"

My whole body deflates. "Yeah." At least Katie and I are in familiar territory again. Parents. Chinese stuff.

"How are you going to explain the Muslim booth to them?"

"Simple—I won't."

She raises an eyebrow. "I don't think you've thought this plan through."

"I have, actually." I take a deep breath. In the last few hours, I've done nothing but think about how to talk to Katie about being Muslim and how to talk to my parents about not doing the Chinese booth. "I don't have to lie to my parents. I'll just ask them to help me practice Chinese calligraphy or whatever, and they'll just assume that I'm doing it for my booth. Problem solved." I don't tell her my other plan: learn to bake traditional pastries eaten at Eid and casually drop questions about being

Chinese Muslim over family dinners. All I really know about being Muslim is that's who we are and—oh yeah—no pork.

Katie shakes her head as she absentmindedly picks up the discarded cracker and pops it into her mouth. "Ugh! Seriously, we need to start that petition." She chews and swallows. "Back to your 'grand plan'"—she pauses to make air quotes—"you know there's, like, a million things wrong with it, right?"

"I know." I fix her with a determined stare. "And there's one more big problem."

She sighs. "I'm afraid to ask, but go ahead. You know I'm in, whatever it is."

I melt in gratitude. "Good. Because we absolutely, positively, can't let Ms. Tucker and my parents come into contact with each other."

Nine

Mom is waiting for me in the entryway when I get home from school. Her job as an accountant lets her work flexible hours, and it's not unusual for her to be home after school, but meeting me at the door with a big grin on her face is definitely different. "I have a wonderful surprise for you."

"Really?" I wonder what it could be. Surprises are usually food with Mom. Did she get us Chinese egg tarts for dessert? I'm already salivating as I imagine the silky egg custard in the flaky pastry cup. Maybe I can slip in a question about which pastries are eaten at Eid. All my parents have told me about Eid is that there's Eid al-Fitr and Eid al-Adha, that they're both feasts, and that Eid al-Fitr is a feast at the end of Ramadan—a month of spirituality and fasting that happens every year in the ninth month of the lunar year. My family doesn't observe Ramadan, though Dad sometimes mentions when it's happening.

I start to take off my shoes to deposit into the shoe tray, but she says, "Keep your shoes on. We're going out." Maybe she's taking us to the little bakery in the strip mall that sells Chinese pastries.

I might be just a tiny bit fixated on egg tarts. I doubt that egg tarts are traditional Eid pastries, but it wouldn't hurt to ask. From what my parents have told me, both of their families celebrated the Islamic holidays when they were growing up. "What kind of pastries did you eat at the Eid feast in Taiwan?"

Mom pauses in the act of reaching for my backpack. "Why do you ask?" She takes my backpack and lets it dangle from her fingertips.

"No reason." It's not like I can say, "I want to know because I accidentally-on-purpose dropped the Chinese booth to do the Muslim booth instead."

"Well," she says, "we didn't eat anything in particular. Just a lot of good food like the kind of meals we have at home to celebrate birthdays and Lunar New Year."

That's not going to work. If I have mooncakes and steamed red bean buns at the Muslim booth, it will be just like the Chinese booth.

Mom is already starting to walk toward my bedroom to deposit my backpack, so I can't ask her any more questions. I guess I'll have to look up traditional Muslim pastries online.

"Where are we going?" I ask when she comes back from my bedroom.

"That's part of the surprise."

All this suspense is making me think it's not egg tarts. And if we're going somewhere without waiting for Dad to come home from work, it's probably not dinner out either. Now I'm starting to get curious. When Mom emerges from my bedroom, I ask, "Does the surprise have anything to do with food?"

"No." She smiles as she slips on her shoes, puts on a jacket, and grabs her purse. "But I think you're going to like it."

As we get into the car, I ask, "Is it bigger than a bread box?"

"I don't even know what a bread box *is*." She buckles her seat belt and glances over to check that I have mine on before starting the engine and pulling out of the driveway. "Is that a white people thing?"

"Maybe." I'm not sure if I've actually ever seen a bread box. It's just a question kids at school ask when we're playing twenty questions. "How about, is it bigger than a loaf of bread?"

She thinks it over. "That depends."

I get in a few more questions as she drives, and I have determined that it's not alive (I guess a puppy was a long shot), it's something I can touch, and I can't play video games on it (game console, also a long shot) before she bans any further questions.

Mom drives us all the way past downtown until we're in a suburb just south of Seattle.

"What are we doing here?" I peer out the window at a sign that says "Great Wall of China Shopping Center" in big red letters. We've been here once or twice before, but it's usually too far for us to go when there are Asian shopping centers closer to us in North Seattle. "I thought you said it wasn't food."

"It's not." She parks, and we get out of the car. "A friend of mine told me about a new store that opened up here."

"Just to be clear," I say, "we're counting egg tarts as food, right? Because I seem to remember that there's a bakery here."

"We can pick up egg tarts when we're done, but that's not the surprise."

Now I'm just *dying* to know.

Mom leads us into the mall and past the main grocery store, a place selling rugs, a bakery, and a boba place. "We're almost there." Her face is shining with excitement. "Close your eyes."

"Do I have to?" But I'm already closing my eyes. My mom's eagerness is contagious. "Okay, my eyes are closed." Anticipation buzzes through me as I put my hands over my eyes for good measure.

"No peeking." She takes my arm and guides me a little farther, and then we make a turn.

"Nǐ hǎo," a voice greets us, probably a store owner.

"Nǐ hǎo," Mom says back.

"Nǐ hǎo." I keep my hands over my eyes, though I feel silly.

"You can look now, Sophie."

I uncover and open my eyes, and I immediately gasp, awe flooding me.

There are racks and racks of silk dresses in vibrant red, deep blue, peach, pink, magenta, emerald, and every other imaginable color. Mannequins by the entrance show off shimmering embroidery of birds, flowers, and dragons on the brilliant colors, and my fingers itch to touch the dresses.

"Are you kidding me?" I shriek, and for once, Mom doesn't tell me to lower my voice. "I can't believe that you're buying me a qípáo!" When I was little, I used to beg my mother to let me wear her wedding qípáo when Katie and I played dress-up, but she always refused. Now I'm getting a qípáo of my own.

She beams at me. "I thought you could pick out one for Katie too. You two are about the same size, and her mother can get it tailored to fit later."

Ah. I get it now. This is Mom's way of apologizing for the birthday party mess, but I'll take a gorgeous qípáo for Katie and me over an "I'm sorry" any day.

"She'll love it," I say confidently. Katie and I used to drape blankets over ourselves and use cardboard, markers, and tape to make a high collar that looked like ones on the qípáos we'd see in movies or in our parents' photo albums.

"The two of you will look so beautiful in your qípáos at the Chinese booth."

Oh, darn. My excitement fizzles away. "Katie's actually not doing the Chinese booth this year." *And neither am I.* "She's doing the LGBTQ+ booth instead."

Mom frowns. "Why can't she do that and the Chinese booth?"

"School rule, I guess. She can only do one booth, and she picked the LGBTQ+ booth."

I swear I didn't mean to make it sound like Katie picked her other friends over me, but Mom's voice is gentle as she says, "That's too bad." She smooths a strand of hair away from my cheek. "But we should still get Katie a traditional Chinese dress. Maybe she'll wear hers at her LGBTQ+ booth, and of course you'll wear yours at the Chinese booth."

A hard knot forms in my stomach. "About that . . ." Katie's right. I'm no good at lying, and I'm going to crack.

Mom doesn't seem to have heard me. She's moved away and is talking to the shop owner. Mom turns to me and holds up an ice-blue shot silk embroidered with silver phoenixes. "What do you think? It's so pretty, but we could go with a bolder color and gold if you want. You don't have to decide right away. Why don't you try on a bunch of them?"

I look at my mother, surrounded by bright silks and so

happy to be giving me this beautiful gift she's looking forward to seeing me wear at the Chinese booth.

How can I throw that back in her face?

"You're right," I tell her. "I don't have to decide yet."

Huh. I sit in bed with my laptop open on my lap. I didn't have a problem finding a bunch of online lists for traditional Eid foods, but there's just one problem. I've never heard of most of them. How am I supposed to run a Muslim booth if I don't even know what kinds of food are eaten on the biggest Islamic holidays? I scroll down one of the lists. Baklava appears on a few of the lists, and at least I've eaten that before at Middle Eastern restaurants. It seems hard to make, but I suppose I have plenty of time to practice in the month before Rainbow Fair.

With a sigh, I close my laptop and flop backward into my Wonder Woman comforter. I'm tempted to do more internet searching on Islam, but it doesn't quite seem right—like I'd be cheating on some kind of "authentic Muslim" test.

"Lights out, Sophie," Dad calls from the hallway.

"Okay. Just a minute." I put my laptop on the nightstand, plug in the charger, and turn off the light, but my mind is still racing. Maybe I'm going about "How to Be an Authentic Muslim in Thirty Days" all wrong. I need to go to the source.

I lie in bed for a few minutes to make sure that Mom and Dad have gone to bed, and when I don't hear anything, I get out of bed and open my bedroom door as quietly as I can. Closing it as silently as I can, I tiptoe downstairs to the bookcase in the corner of the living room.

Mystery novel, dictionary, romance . . . ah, there it is, or rather, there *they* are. Two thick books with dark blue covers and gold scrolling designs on the spines are sitting on the top shelf. Our family's Quran. But I never wondered before why there are two copies. I take one of the Qurans from the bookshelf, but on the cover, the words are all in Arabic and Chinese. I don't know any Arabic and am not much better when it comes to reading in Chinese. I replace it on the shelf and take down the second one. Unlike the other Quran, this one has a dusty cover. It also has Arabic writing in gold on the cover but with an English translation. *The Holy Quran.* The word "holy" does something funny to my heart.

The Quran isn't a reference book for a school project. It's a *religious* text. I may have been Muslim all my life, but what does that mean when I know next to nothing about Islam?

Maybe I don't have the right to read this book.

Carefully, I wipe off some of the dust before returning the Arabic-English Quran to the bookshelf.

Ten

"Tonight is the first hurdle," I tell Katie the next day as we're walking back to my house. I invited her over so Mom and I can give her the qípáo I picked out for her.

"What do you mean?" Katie asks.

"It's Parent-Teacher Curriculum Night," I say. When she just stares at me with a blank expression, I say impatiently, "Ms. Tucker is going to go right up to my parents and tell them how *thrilled* she is that I'm running a Muslim booth this year, and then my parents will know that I'm not doing the Chinese booth."

Understanding dawns on Katie's face. "Oh, right. We can't let that happen. But I've got to admit—I'm surprised you haven't already told your parents everything."

She's not the only one. I was sure I'd spill my guts to my parents about switching booths too, but then Mom took me shopping for qípáos, reminding me how important the Chinese booth is to my parents. She didn't blink at paying full price, not even grumbling under her breath in Chinese like she usually does. In this case, the shopkeeper would have understood, but Mom genuinely didn't seem to care about how much money she spent.

And Dad didn't ask how much the qípáo cost when I modeled it at home. I seriously can't remember the last time my parents didn't complain about the price of anything they didn't get at a bargain. "As far as my parents know, I'm doing the Chinese booth, and it has to stay that way."

Katie puts her arm through mine. "Okay, I've got you. We have to keep Ms. Tucker and your parents so distracted that they won't have time to talk to each other."

"Any ideas?"

She thinks for a bit. "I can come up with a Rainbow Fair crisis that keeps Ms. Tucker busy. Let's put together a top ten list of things the steering committee has turned down, and I'll get the LGBTQ+ booth to propose them all tonight. The dunk tank idea alone should keep her occupied. Especially if we ask her to be in the tank."

"Don't go overboard," I say hastily.

"If you think that's overboard," Katie says, "then you're definitely not going to like my idea for how to keep your parents distracted."

"I'm afraid to ask." What can be worse than suggesting

students dunk our Rainbow Fair faculty advisor into a tank of icy water?

"Okay, just hear me out," she begins, and now I'm *really* worried. I have a vague memory that the roller derby idea started with Katie asking me to hear her out.

"You could tell your parents you're getting a B in a class," she says, speaking so fast her words tumble over each other.

For a second, I don't think I heard her right because, of course, she couldn't possibly be proposing anything so preposterous. Then my brain catches up with me, and I realize that she *did* just say that. I gape at her, and my whole body freezes like I'm the one who's just been dunked into a tank of cold water. "You can't be serious."

"I know! I know! But it would work."

"Katie," I say, trying to keep my voice from turning into a shriek, "the plan is to distract my parents—not give them a heart attack." I might be exaggerating a bit, but my parents are sure to think something is wrong with me if I told them I was getting a B in a class. They'll freak out, and I'm talking ginger tea with lemon and "cold washcloth on my head" treatment.

"How about a B-plus?" she suggests.

I shake my head. "Still 'Asian D' territory."

"A-minus, then, and maybe in an elective class like art?"

I pause. That might downgrade the tea and washcloth panic into just enough concern to keep my parents distracted, but it still seems extreme. "I'm getting an A-plus in art," I protest.

"Would you prefer telling your parents that you're getting an A-minus in math instead?"

"Point taken." I sigh. "Can we put an A-minus in art into the last-resort category and keep trying to think of a better idea?"

"Fine. But I don't think we're going to come up with anything else to stop your parents from insisting on talking to every single one of your teachers, and that includes Ms. Tucker."

I have a sinking feeling that she's right.

Dad takes another picture of Katie and me in front of a big banner that says, "Welcome to Monroe Middle School Parent-Teacher Curriculum Night." Students are showing their parents their classrooms, but we haven't made it past the school's entryway because our families are too caught up in taking pictures of us. Or at least my parents are.

"You realize that this is just Parent-Teacher Curriculum Night and nothing special, right?" I ask.

"It doesn't hurt to get a few pictures when you're both dressed up." Mom smiles. "I can't wait to see you both wearing your qípáos."

"That was too generous of you," Ms. Yang says.

"It's so beautiful!" Katie's eyes are shining. "Thank you so much, Ms. Hu."

"Are you sure we can't pay you for the dress?" Mr. Yang asks.

"Nonsense," Mom and Dad say at the same time.

Mom presses Ms. Yang's hand. "Our girls have been friends for the longest time. It wouldn't be right to get Sophie a qípáo without giving Katie one too."

This is Mom's way of smoothing over the awkwardness at the birthday sleepover breakfast. Gifts are definitely Mom's love language.

"It's too bad they won't both be in the Chinese booth this year," she adds.

"Mom," I mutter, my face growing hot. I know Mom is supportive of the LGBTQ+ booth, so that's not why she can't let go of the fact that Katie isn't going to do the Chinese booth this year. How is she going to react when she finds out her own daughter isn't doing it either?

To my surprise, Mr. Yang is nodding in agreement. "It really is a shame."

"It's not like I *wanted* to drop the Chinese booth." Katie frowns. "But like I told you, the school doesn't allow us to do more than one booth."

Ms. Yang gives her husband a pointed look and puts her arm around Katie's shoulders. "We're both very proud of you for establishing the very first LGBTQ+ booth."

"Of course," he says hastily. "Very proud."

"Wonderful accomplishment," my dad says, like Katie had won the spelling bee.

"Absolutely." Mom nods. "I'm just saying it's too bad you can't do both, Katie. I know Sophie will miss having you in the Chinese booth."

I don't hear Katie's response because all sound is suddenly sucked away when I spot Ms. Tucker bearing down on us with a huge grin on her face. Frantically, I grab Katie's arm, and she takes in the situation with a single glance.

"Sorry," she says calmly, "but I need to ask Ms. Tucker a question." Smooth as the silk in her new qípáo, she intercepts Ms. Tucker with her parents behind her. "Just the teacher I wanted to see," she sings out. "What do you think of our booth having a dunk tank?"

Ms. Tucker's eyebrows rise into her hairline. "Oh, I don't think that's a—"

"Maybe we should find the others to see what they think of a dunk tank. I have some other ideas too. These are my parents, by the way." Katie is steering Ms. Tucker away from my parents and me as she talks.

Wow. My best friend is eerily good at this spy stuff. I'm glad she's on my side.

"Isn't that your English teacher?" Dad asks, making my heart race again.

"And the Rainbow Fair Committee chair," Mom adds. "We should go talk to her."

Utterly panicked, I blurt out, "I'm getting an A-minus in art!"

For a long moment, neither parent says anything. Then, in a calm voice reserved for only the most dire of emergencies, my father says, "We'll get through this, Sophie. It's going to be okay."

Their reaction totally tracks, but *come on*. I told them I got an A-minus in a class—not that I have an incurable disease.

"I'm sure we can figure something out." Mom doesn't sound as calm as Dad, but her Mom-on-a-mission voice isn't any better. "Let's go talk to your art teacher and see if there's anything you can do to raise your grade."

Ms. Miller is going to be *so* confused. She gives everyone an A-plus just for doing the work.

Darn that Katie Yang for coming up with this plan. "Isn't it enough that I tried my best?" I ask desperately.

"Of course," Mom says, "and that's the point. You tried your best, and your efforts should be acknowledged."

Ms. Miller would be the first to agree. She told me that my blobby, lopsided drawing of a horse showed "imagination and originality."

Left with no other choice, I drag my feet as I show my parents the way to the art classroom. "There's just one thing," I say. "You can't mention the A-minus. I'm not supposed to know."

Dad frowns. "You're not supposed to know your own grade?"

Right. I did not think that through. "Well, I kind of overheard her talking about . . . um, grades and stuff . . . to someone." I cringe even as I'm speaking. No, not super vague at all. I'm clearly not made for a life of crime.

"I'm not sure I understand," Mom says, but Dad puts his hand on my shoulder.

"We won't mention the A-minus if you don't want us to," he says gently.

There are cold washcloths and ginger tea in my future for sure.

Ms. Miller is gushing over some other kid's art project when we enter the classroom, but she pauses to smile at me. "Sophie! I'll be over to talk to you and your parents in just a moment. I can't wait to show them the horse you drew!"

"I think this is going to go well," Mom whispers to me on one side.

"See? Nothing to worry about," Dad whispers on my other side.

Now I feel even worse. Not only am I lying to my parents, but Ms. Miller is going to think my parents are some kind of Asian tiger-parent stereotype who are pushing me too hard.

Is it weird that they're panicking over a mythical A-minus? Well, yes.

But it's not that simple.

Mom is always telling me I shouldn't settle, and Dad is always telling me that I can do anything. So this whole messy plan to keep them from finding out about the Chinese booth isn't because I'm afraid they're going to ground me for life or yell at me or any of the awful stuff I see Asian parents do on TV.

I just don't want to let them down or have them think I'm not proud to be Chinese.

Eleven

I open my laptop and wriggle into the pillows cushioning the headboard of my bed. It's crunch time. It's been a week since I've been assigned to the Muslim booth, and my Chinese calligraphy is improving, but that won't help me with the booth I'm actually running. And Rainbow Fair is only three weeks away.

My mouth tightens as I search for "Chinese Muslims" online. The first thing that comes up is an unfamiliar word. "Hui," I say out loud, and the word is both awkward and familiar. It's the word I know for gray, but Mandarin is full of one-syllable words, so lots of words sound the same.

I read more and find out there are different ethnic groups in China. "Han" is the word for the main Chinese ethnic group, but there are many others, including Hui and other Muslim ethnic groups. "Hui" is actually the word used to mean "Chinese Muslim."

I stop reading and take a deep breath. This is a lot. I don't know if I'm Hui or some other ethnicity. My parents have only ever said we're Muslim, and I thought it was as simple as that. I never imagined there would be *different* kinds of Chinese Muslims.

I open a new document on my laptop and start taking notes on all this.

"Sophie," my dad calls out from somewhere in the house. "We're starting the show. Are you coming?"

I glance at the time. I've been up here an hour working on my Muslim booth notes. "Coming!" I yell, closing my laptop. I have to admit that this part of my parents' Chinese booth prep is inspired. For the past week, we've been watching a fifty-hour wǔxiá miniseries they both used to watch in Taiwan. I'm so hooked on the cool martial arts fighting and heart-wrenching drama that I don't even care if they're sneaking in language and history lessons during the show.

I grab my notebook and a pen as I leave my bedroom. It's weird how much my Muslim research overlaps with my Chinese research. I glance at the scribbles in my notebook about Chinese ethnic groups and different dynasties. Maybe it's not so strange after all. Like I told Katie when she asked me how I can be both Chinese and Muslim—that's just who I am.

I close the notebook and run into the living room. "Don't start without me!"

"Like we would do that." Mom passes me the popcorn as I squeeze past the TV trays to sit down between my parents on the couch. Dad gives me a small bowl for my popcorn.

I put the notebook in my lap and use the cup in the popcorn bowl to fill up my own bowl. "Okay, I'm ready." I don't actually take notes during the show, but sometimes I'll write down something afterward.

My dad starts the DVD because this show is so old that it's not available for streaming. We had left off on a cliff-hanger. A mysterious masked assassin has been murdering members of the martial arts sect led by Qiao Feng, the main character, and as he's looking for the assassin, he finds out that his adoptive parents aren't his real ones. He's just about to find out the secret of his birth.

On-screen, a dramatic announcement is made, and suddenly the members of the clan are accusing their own leader of being the assassin, and they're all fighting.

I actually drop my popcorn. "Wait. I don't get it. Why do they think Qiao Feng is the assassin?"

My parents are used to explaining the parts I don't always catch because of my limited Chinese, but this time, they hesitate.

"Remember we told you that this takes place at a time in

Chinese history when there were many warring kingdoms?" Mom asks.

I nod. I don't have to open up my notebook to remember that.

"Well," Dad says, "it's even more complicated than that. The kingdoms are all part of larger empires, and there are two empires trying to rule China—the Song and the Liao. The clan is part of the Song, and Qiao Feng's birth parents are of the Liao empire."

"I still don't get it." I point at the screen where his clan is literally turning their backs on Qiao Feng. "They're treating him as if he's guilty, and they have no proof!" Wasn't he raised by the clan from when he was a baby? Why would it matter where his birth parents are from?

On-screen, Qiao Feng stumbles away from his clan, tears off the badge that marks him as a member, and shouts, "I am a Qidan person!"

Qidan. That sounds strangely familiar. "What does that mean? 'Qidan'?"

"The Song are the Han people, but the Liao are the Qidan," Dad says. "That's like us, actually."

In the banishment scene, it's raining now, and Qiao Feng has been cast out from a clan without a single friend he's known from childhood willing to believe in his innocence.

My heart clenches, and I open my notebook. Here it is. *Qidan*. I wrote it down next to the more commonly known name of Khitan, and yes, these were the people of the Khitan Empire, also known as the Liao dynasty.

"So are we Khitan, then? I mean, are we Qidan?"

Dad shakes his head. "Oh no. We're not Qidan people. I just meant that we're not Han. That's the main Chinese ethnic group."

"Your dad means that we're outsiders like the Qidan people," Mom adds.

"So we're huī, then?"

Dad hits pause on the remote, freezing Qiao Feng's look of agony. Mom looks at me blankly.

"Huī," I say again. "Chinese Muslim?"

"Oh." Mom laughs. "I thought you were asking if we're the color gray!"

That's the not-so-fun part of Chinese. If I don't pronounce a word exactly right, it could end up meaning something completely different.

"It's pronounced like the 'huí' in 'huí jiā,'" she says. *Return home.*

"Huí," I say again, pronouncing it to mean "return," which has a little more of a lilt than the word for "gray." Both words sound like I'm saying "hway," but the tiny difference in how I say it changes the meaning completely.

"That's right," Mom says, "and yes, we are Hui. But it's more accurate to say 'Huímín.' That means 'Hui people.'"

"So I can say we're Huímín?"

She nods. "Yes, that way others will know what you mean." By "others," she means Chinese people. I'm pretty sure the typical Rainbow Fair crowd won't know the difference, but I write down "Huímín" in my notebook anyway.

"How did you hear of Hui?" Dad asks.

"I've been researching Chinese history for the Rainbow Fair booth." Not a lie, although I'm careful not to say *which* booth.

Dad's eyes brighten. "Well, if you're interested in our family's history, I can tell you that we have roots in Xixia, although that's not where we're originally from." He has a master's in Chinese history and wanted to be a professor, but no one would hire a teacher with an accent or with such specialized knowledge. That's why he went to community college to get an IT degree. But Dad still loves to explain this kind of stuff. "I can trace my ancestry all the way to the Ottoman Empire—in an area that's now modern-day Turkey."

"My side of the family doesn't have that kind of record-keeping," Mom says with a smile at Dad. "I just know we're also from Xixia."

I'm flipping through my notebook. "Is Xixia the Western Xia dynasty?" From what I can tell, dynasties mean ruling family, time period, and empire. My forehead wrinkles. So—not confusing at all.

"That's right." Dad leans toward me, so excited that he spills some popcorn and doesn't seem to realize it. "Xixia was a dynasty lasting from the eleventh to the early thirteenth century. The Silk Road, which connected northeastern China with central Asia, ran through Xixia. Many immigrants settled in Xixia at that time."

I'm writing down everything he says, but I'm not sure what use this will be. I'm just trying to pull out something clear I can use for the Muslim booth, and all this is hard for me to wrap my head around.

"It's wonderful that you're interested in our family history." Dad is smiling at me.

"You know," Mom says, a gleam in her eye, "they do teach history in Chinese school."

I slam my notebook shut. "Let's not get carried away."

Dad laughs. "I was the same way at your age."

Yeah, right. "It's not like you had to go to Saturday English school in Taiwan." Both my parents were born in Taiwan, but they still think of themselves as Chinese too.

"Of course not," he says. "We learned English in our regular classes. No, I'm talking about Arabic Saturday school."

I stare at him in surprise. "You speak Arabic, Dad?"

"Not as well as I'd like, but the Quran is written in Arabic, you know, and our prayers are in Arabic."

"I never learned," Mom says wistfully. "There aren't as many Muslims in Taiwan. I guess we were outsiders there too." Her eyes lock onto me. "When you're older, you'll be glad you went to Chinese school even if it was just for a few years."

"Can't I just watch a bunch of wǔxiá shows to learn Chinese?" I pick up the remote sitting on Dad's TV tray. "We still have, like, forty hours left of this one."

"Fine." Her mouth twitches up in a smile. "I suppose I should just be glad you're interested in the show."

"And that you're working so hard on the Chinese booth," Dad adds. "We're so proud of you."

The popcorn turns into a leaden lump in my stomach. "Thanks," I mutter as I press play.

Qiao Feng beats his chest in his grief and proceeds to wander the stormy plains, friendless and uncertain of who he really is.

I know how you feel, buddy.

Twelve

I dodge around other students during the study period as I hurry down the hall to the LGBTQ+ Student Union room. Today is an "allies welcome" meeting, and I promised Katie I'd come.

"Sophie," Ms. Terrence, the seventh-grade counselor, calls out. "Do you have a moment?"

I don't really, but I can't say that with Ms. Terrence staring at me intensely with concern in her light gray eyes. What is this about? "Um, sure."

"I just had a chat with Ms. Miller, and I was wondering how you're doing. Any stress or pressure you want to talk about?"

Oh no. My body seizes up. This is about my parents at the Parent-Teacher Curriculum Night badgering Ms. Miller about extra-credit art projects and talking about how much effort I put into the lopsided horse drawing. "I'm not feeling any stress." I smile weakly. "Um, thanks for checking?"

"Everything okay at home?"

"Great. Couldn't be better." That's not exactly true, but it's not because my parents are locking me in my bedroom to do homework, if that's what she's thinking. It's because my lies about my grades have dramatically backfired. I kept Ms. Tucker and my parents from talking, but now people think my parents are super strict and obsessed with my grades.

"Well, if you need to talk, you know where to find me." Ms. Terrence smiles sympathetically, and my gut tightens.

"I'm good." I back away. "I need to get to a club meeting."

"Of course. I won't keep you."

I can feel her worried eyes on my back as I rush off.

My encounter with Ms. Terrence has made me late, and I'm out of breath by the time I fling open the door to the club room.

Is it my imagination or did everyone stop talking when I walked in? And why is everyone staring at me? Katie, Shane, Megan, and Allie are all sitting in a circle of chairs.

"Sophie," Katie says, her voice a little too bright. "I'm glad you're here."

Allie and Megan exchange glances, and Shane has a strange, anxious expression on their face.

"Hi, Sophie," Shane says, and their voice is also a little too something as well.

I walk over to the four of them, trying to catch my breath

and figure out what the heck is going on. Should I pretend I don't notice anything weird? I catch Katie's eye, and she motions to the empty chair next to her. "Sit here, Sophie." There's a tense line on her forehead.

I go over to the empty chair but don't sit down. "Um, did I mix up the meetings?" The club has meetings that are just for students who identify as LGBTQ+, and I'm suddenly worried that I've accidentally crashed that one. "I can go if I'm not supposed to be here."

"No," Katie and Shane say at the same time.

"You didn't mix up the meetings," Shane says with a smile.

Allie and Megan don't say anything, but Katie reaches over and gives Megan a not-so-subtle nudge.

"Right," Megan says quickly. "It's all good, Sophie." She elbows Allie.

Seriously. What the heck?

"Okay, if no one else is going to say it, I will." Allie folds her arms. "We're just wondering—"

"Stop it." Katie's voice is sharp.

"*You're* the only one wondering, Allie," Shane adds. "Don't speak for the rest of us."

Wondering what? A sour lump forms in my throat.

"All right." Allie doesn't meet my eyes, and the sick feeling in my body gets worse. "Sophie, I heard your religion believes in stoning gays. So I'm wondering how you can be Muslim and be friends with us."

My mouth drops open, and there's a pounding in my ears. I'm suddenly right back in second grade when a kid confronted Katie and me during lunch. *Do Chinese people really eat dogs?*

That time, Katie had shoved that kid so hard that he fell down, clutching his skinned knees and moaning like she had tried to murder him. He put on such a convincing performance that Katie got suspended for fighting despite the huge fuss her parents raised about double standards and how the other kid didn't get disciplined at all. I didn't think it was fair either. If Katie was in trouble for standing up against the racism we both experienced, then I should have been in trouble as well. No one else seemed to agree. Despite my pleading, our principal refused to suspend me too. But the point is that Katie and I are always on each other's side. Except now, Katie is just sitting there, pale and silent.

I don't know if my best friend is on my side this time.

I'm on my own. My body feels like it's being squeezed tight, and before I know it, I'm taking a step toward Allie. Her eyes widen, and she scrambles to her feet like she thinks I'm going to push her chair over with her in it, but that's not my style.

Katie is staring at me with her face all flushed. I can't tell what she's thinking. Pain stabs into my heart. I *always* used to know what she's thinking. And I might not be able to read Katie, but the defiant anger on Allie's face is clear, and so are the conflicted feelings in Megan's expression and the worry in Shane's eyes.

The way they're looking at me—this is part of why I didn't talk about being Muslim. Maybe it wasn't the whole truth when I told Katie I wasn't trying to keep being Muslim a secret. It's true that I'm not ashamed of who I am, but I also know people see us as dangerous. I think of my parents telling me that we're outsiders because we're Hui. Outsiders in China, in Taiwan, and now—here in the United States too.

Anger flares in me, and now I'm thinking of a different moment—two years ago when some kid had confronted Katie and me on the playground. *Hey, Chinese virus—go back home!* Heat licks at my stomach. "Do you want to blame me for the coronavirus while you're at it, Allie?"

"That's totally not the same!" Allie sputters. "Are you calling me a racist?"

Yeah, actually. You're a racist, Allie. The words are on the tip of my tongue, but Megan speaks before I can.

"Allie didn't mean it like that," Megan says, her eyes darting between Allie and me. "She was just asking a question."

Are you a dog-eater? Did you cause the pandemic? Those are all questions too.

Katie leaps to her feet. "Allie, you need to apologize to Sophie." Her voice is hard, and my heart beats with painful relief. "And, Megan, don't defend her."

Katie didn't hit the kid who called us "Chinese virus," but she did use impressively creative profanity. That time, she didn't get suspended, but she did get what our school called restorative justice. I was restorative-justiced too, and it was basically the other kid defending his racism and getting "heard." Katie said she would have preferred getting suspended again to sitting in a room with a bunch of adults sympathizing with this kid and trying to get us to see "his side." I wonder if that's what she's thinking of now.

"Sophie is my best friend." Katie clenches her fingers as she faces Allie and Megan. "She's not suddenly a different person, and she doesn't deserve to be treated this way."

Megan bites her lip. "I'm sorry, Sophie."

"I'm sorry too," Shane says, even though they didn't do anything, but maybe that's what they're apologizing for.

Allie drops her gaze. "Sorry, Sophie," she mumbles.

"It's okay." It's not, but they are Katie's friends. My eyes stay on her. *She's* the one I care about.

It feels like we're back on the same side, but there's still a tightness in my chest. Katie might be standing up for me now, but she can't really understand what it's like for everyone to make assumptions about me because I'm Muslim. Just like I can't understand what it's like for her to deal with homophobia. But Katie has her other friends who do get it.

I don't have anyone.

Thirteen

My stomach lurches when I'm called to the counselor's office during art class. Ms. Terrence must be following up on our hallway "Is everything okay at home?" chat. I never should have started down this path of lies.

I leave the classroom and drag my feet all the way to Ms. Terrence's office. I'll just have to do better at convincing my counselor that my parents aren't making me do twelve hours of homework a day and forcing me to go without food or sleep unless I get perfect grades. It really shouldn't be this hard to prove something that's actually true.

I take a deep breath and knock on the door.

"Come in!" Ms. Terrence doesn't sound too stressed, so maybe this won't be so bad.

I inhale and open the door.

Ms. Terrence isn't alone. A girl is sitting in a chair across from my counselor's desk, and there's an empty chair next to her. The girl has a friendly face and dark brown eyes that are peering at me with curiosity.

Maybe this isn't a follow-up to our hallway conversation after all.

"Sophie," Ms. Terrence says with a big smile, "I'd like you to meet Anna Demir. She's a transfer student."

"Hi, Sophie," Anna says.

"Hi," I say, still not sure what's happening.

Ms. Terrence motions for me to sit, and I take a seat on the chair next to Anna.

"I was thinking you could show Anna around. She's in some of the same classes you are."

I can't be the only one who shares classes with her, so why me? I don't ask this question out loud. "Yeah, sure."

"Are you the one running the Muslim booth?" Anna asks with a smile.

I blink at her. "Yes." Why is she asking?

"I should have mentioned the good news first." Ms. Terrence beams at us both. "You're no longer running the Muslim booth all by yourself, Sophie. Anna will be joining you."

Understanding comes over me. Anna is Muslim.

I smile weakly. "That's awesome."

"Assalamu alaikum." Anna looks at me like she's expecting me to say something back, but I have no idea what she said, much less what I'm supposed to say in response.

My hands go damp. "Um, yeah. Nice to meet you."

Anna's eyebrows draw together, but she doesn't comment.

"School's almost out for today," Ms. Terrence says. "Sophie, why don't you take Anna to the library after you show her around? The two of you can start working together on the Muslim booth."

Anna's eyes light up. "I would love that!" She actually looks like she means it. "I have so many ideas."

I'll bet she does. Another realization hits me then, this time with all the force of a flash flood, and my body goes cold all over. My panicked research into Islam might be good enough for the rest of Monroe Middle School, but Anna will see me for who I am, and *not* in a good way. I didn't even know how to return her greeting.

The only thing worse than being the school's only Muslim is being the school's inauthentic Muslim.

"Ms. Tucker, the Rainbow Fair advisor, will be happy to have you join us," Ms. Terrence says.

That's an understatement. If Ms. Tucker was glad to have *me* run the Muslim booth, she's going to practically melt with joy when she meets Anna.

"I know you must be eager to get started." Ms. Terrence stands, and Anna and I do too. "Have fun, girls."

"You've probably already done a lot of work on the booth,"

Anna says to me as we're walking out of Ms. Terrence's office. "So please tell me to back off if I overwhelm you with too many new ideas. I just get excited about this kind of thing."

Excited about a Rainbow Fair booth? Yeah, Ms. Tucker is going to *love* her.

"That's fine." I shove my hands into the pockets of my hoodie. "I, uh, haven't done a lot of work on the booth yet."

"It must be hard to run a booth all by yourself," she says, following me down the hallway. "I'll be happy to help."

"Thanks." I wish I could return her friendliness, but I'm just too freaked out about being discovered as a fraud. I gesture toward the glass windows of the library as we pass it. "Here's the library."

She peers at the colorful displays of books in the window. "Your school is so much nicer than my last one."

"So where are you from?" I come to a halt in the middle of the hallway. I didn't mean it to come out that way. "Sorry! I mean, what *middle school* are you from? Not what country." The words tumble quickly out of my mouth. "I hate the 'where are you from' question, and that's not what I meant." *Stop talking, Sophie.* For once, my inner voice cuts through my panicked babbling, and I stop. At least the hallway is empty so no one else but Anna is witness to my social awkwardness.

She smiles. "I transferred here from a school in California

because my dad got a job in Seattle. I was born in California, but my parents are from Turkey."

"That's cool." I think of my father telling me he can trace our family ancestry to what is now Turkey. I want to share this with Anna, but what if it sounds like I'm reaching for a connection?

Anna cocks her head to the side. "Why do you hate the 'where are you from' question?"

She asks it so naturally that I answer before I stop to think. "Because it makes me feel like I'm being asked if I belong. Like the person asking assumes I don't belong here—in the United States."

"But you weren't questioning my belonging when you asked me where I'm from." Her voice is matter-of-fact.

"Of course not!"

"So is it okay to ask you questions about you and your family?" She smiles again. "Mom says I ask too many personal questions, but I'm just always curious about people, and I want to get to know you."

I can't help but smile back. I like Anna's directness. "Sure."

"Good. If we're going to work on the Muslim booth together, we should get to know each other."

My skin turns clammy. I know I'm being paranoid, but I have this awful feeling I'm going to do something totally ignorant. I can already see that friendly look in Anna's eyes turn to disappointment.

The bell rings, signaling the end of school, and doors burst open all down the hallway, followed by students streaming out of their classrooms.

"Should we get started on our booth planning now?" Anna has to raise her voice to be heard over the chatter and shouts of the other kids.

I wish I could say that I had to go home, but I'd already told my parents I was staying after school to do Chinese booth planning. "Yeah, let me get my backpack from art class."

"Sophie!" Katie's voice calls out. "Wait up."

I glance back to see her weaving between other students to get to me. When she finally reaches me, she's flushed and breathless. Her forehead knits together when her gaze lands on Anna.

"Hi, Katie," I say. "This is Anna. She's a new student who just transferred from a school in California. Anna, this is my friend Katie."

"Hi, Anna." Katie pauses to catch her breath. "Welcome to Monroe Middle School."

"Thanks." Anna flashes a wide smile. "Everyone has been so nice. I'm sure I'll like it here."

Katie smiles back, but I can tell she doesn't know how to

react to Anna's sunny optimism. "Can I borrow Sophie for a minute?"

"No problem," Anna says, but Katie barely waits for an answer before pulling me aside.

"Listen," she says, "I'm really sorry about earlier today. I talked to Allie again, and she promises that she'll do better."

My heart lifts. "Thanks for talking to Allie." It means a lot to me that Katie would make sure I feel safe around her other friends.

"I also told the others that I'm taking a break from the booth today to spend some time with you. Can we go get some froyo, just the two of us?"

"Sure—Oh darn! I can't." My heart plummets. There's nothing I want more than frozen yogurt with Katie, but I can't just ditch Anna.

"Why not?"

"I have to work on the Muslim booth."

Katie laughs, clearly thinking I'm joking. "Good one, Sophie."

"No, I'm serious," I say reluctantly. "I promised Anna that we'd start planning."

The amusement dies from her eyes. "Oh. So Anna is Muslim?"

"Yeah."

"Can't you, um . . ." She drops her voice to a whisper. "Work on the booth with Anna some other time?" She doesn't add that *she's* ditching the LGBTQ+ booth for me, but I can tell she's thinking it.

I'm tempted. I really am. Katie has been spending so much time with her other friends that it seems like forever since it's just been the two of us. But then I glance over at Anna, patiently waiting for me in the middle of the hall while students push past her on their way to the exit. "I'm sorry," I tell Katie, "but I can't."

"Fine." Katie's tone is as cool as the froyo we're both missing out on. "I guess I'll tell the others I'm available after all."

Wait! Come back! I've changed my mind. But I don't call after my best friend as she walks away from me.

Instead, I go back to Anna. "Let's get started on research for the Muslim booth."

Fourteen

The doorbell rings, and I wipe my sticky hands on my apron. Perfect timing. It took me two hours, but Anna and I will be able to taste-test the baklava for our second planning meeting.

I frown at my reflection as I pass the hall mirror. There's phyllo dough on my cheek and what might be honey in my hair. Not exactly the image I wanted to project, especially since our first planning session consisted of Anna making plans and me pretending I understood more than half of what she suggested. My sole contribution was the baklava.

I fling open the door to Anna's trademark smile.

"Assalamu alaikum," she says, just like she did when we met in Ms. Terrence's office.

This time I know what it means. According to the frantic internet search I did, it's an Arabic phrase that means "Peace be upon you," and it's a greeting Muslims say to each other. I now know I'm supposed to return the greeting with a phrase that means "And unto you peace" but in Arabic. I take a deep breath, but my mouth goes dry. The problem is—despite listening to pronunciation videos over and over again, I'm 100 percent positive that I would flub it.

"Come on in!" I say instead.

"It's so nice of you to have me over." Anna holds out a white box of chocolates and doesn't seem to notice my epic fail. "My parents told me to give this to you." Her parents must be a lot like mine.

I take the box from her, relieved that she didn't denounce me as a bad Muslim when I didn't greet her properly. "Thanks." I told my parents I was doing Rainbow Fair prep but didn't tell them a friend was coming over. If I tell them Anna came and brought a gift, they'll assume she's Chinese and will ask all kinds of questions about her family. They would probably want to meet her too. *I guess I'm eating these chocolates on my own.*

Anna comes inside and sniffs the air. "What's that smell?"

I smell it too. A burnt-sugar scent, sharp and strong. The baklava. *That's not good.* Heart thumping, I race back to the kitchen, toss the chocolates on the table, and yank open a drawer for the oven mitts.

Anna has followed me in. "Can I help?"

"No," I say sadly, pulling the pan of sticky, burnt pastry from the oven. "I think it's too late."

I put the pan on the stovetop, and we both stare at the lumpy squares. Even if they weren't burnt on top, the baklava does not look like the perfect thin layers filled with ground pistachios shown on the online recipe.

"I bet we can still eat them if we scrape the burned bits from the top," Anna says. "Um, can I ask what they're supposed to be?"

"Baklava."

"That's hard to make." She sounds sympathetic.

Great. It would have been nice to know that before I tried to make it.

"My family just gets ours as takeout. Does your family usually make your own baklava?"

"Um, no." I grab a spatula and scrape up a piece of charred pastry to avoid looking at her. "This is my first try."

"That's so cool you tried to make baklava! Where does your family usually buy it from?"

I drop the spatula and face her. This failed baking attempt was my contribution to the Muslim booth, and it doesn't even have anything to do with Islam. It's time to stop pretending that I'm someone I'm not. I take a breath. "I've only had it a few times, actually."

Anna doesn't miss a beat. "Then I'll bring you some when I come over again or when you come to my house."

That went better than I thought. At least she didn't immediately accuse me of being a poser. The tightness in my shoulders eases a bit. "Yeah, that would be great. Thanks."

Anna goes over to the pan of baklava and peels off the top burnt layer of one of the squares of pastry. "This doesn't look too bad." She uses the spatula to cut off a small piece and starts eating it.

"How is it?" I ask anxiously.

She chews slowly and swallows. "Well, it's different. . . ."

Uh-oh. I cut off another piece and brace myself before I pop it into my mouth. Sharp nuts stab into my tongue, and a charred sweetness fills my mouth. "Just checking, this doesn't taste like any baklava you've ever had, right?"

"No, not even close."

We look at each other and start laughing.

"Did you ground up the pistachios at all?" she asks, tears streaming from her eyes with laughter.

"I kind of pounded them with a spoon?"

She shakes her head. "I think maybe you shouldn't try to bake anything else for our booth."

My laughter dies, and a hard knot forms in my chest. "The thing is . . . I'm not sure *what* I can bring to the booth."

She looks at me, her face puzzled. "What do you mean?"

"Well, my family doesn't really practice all that much. I

mean, when you greeted me, I knew I was supposed to greet you back, but I just didn't know how to say it." I hesitate, but she just stays quiet and watches me like she's focusing on my words. I stop but then force myself to push the words past my dry throat. "I'm not sure I'm a real Muslim."

"Sophie," Anna says gently, taking my sticky hands in hers. "There's more than one way to be Muslim."

Warm wetness stings the back of my eyes. "So you're not going to kick me out of your booth?"

Anna laughs. "No, I'm not going to kick you out of *our* booth." She pauses. "And, Sophie?"

"Yes?" I'm trying to sneakily wipe my eyes on my apron. "You want me to promise never to make baklava again? Done. You don't have to worry about that."

"That's not what I was going to say." Her expression is serious.

The hem of the apron drops from my nerveless hands as I stare at her.

"You don't have to say 'Assalamu alaikum' to me or say 'Wa alaikum as-salam' back to me, but I'm going to still greet you the way I would any Muslim because that's who you are. Of course you're a real Muslim."

Anna is looking at me as if she can see all the way into me, and my heart balloons into something big and light.

✦

We're in Anna's bedroom after school the next day when a ding goes off on her phone.

I look up from my laptop, where I'm doing more research on the Hui people. "What's that?"

She reaches over to silence the notification on her phone. "It's time for Maghrib." Taking in my confused look, she explains, "It's the sunset prayer. You can join me if you want."

I look out her bedroom window and see that the light is fading to dark in the sky. Shyness clogs my throat, but I make myself say, "I don't know what to do."

"I can show you." Quickly, she adds, "But only if you want to. No pressure."

The thing is—I really want to learn. Anna hasn't made me feel bad for not knowing much about Islam so far, and I trust her. "I do want to."

Her face lights up in a smile. "The first thing we do is wudu. It's the cleansing ritual we do before prayer."

"Wudu. Got it." I get off her bed and follow Anna out of her bedroom. My parents have told me about the cleansing before prayer, but I didn't know it was called wudu. "My parents say they both had a kettle or something they used when they were little."

Anna smiles. "Yeah, I just use the bathroom sink." We

go into the bathroom, and she tells me to set my intention to pray and then say "Bismillah," telling me I can say it silently if I want.

"Bismillah," I repeat after her, and the word is both unfamiliar and soothing on my tongue.

Then she turns on the faucet and shows me what to wash and how many times. I splash cool water over my hands, into my mouth and nose, my face, arms, head, ears, and feet. I don't know how I'll ever remember the order, but Anna says she'll write it down for me or I can look it up online.

We go back to her bedroom, and Anna takes out two headscarves. She hands me one, a long peach-colored cloth that feels soft and silky in my hands. Then she covers her hair with a blue scarf.

Clumsily, I put the scarf over my head and wrap the ends around my neck. "Like this?" I ask.

"That's fine," she says encouragingly.

It is fine, and that's true in more ways than one. I spread out the prayer rug next to Sophie, and then I follow her motions without trying to repeat the Arabic words of the prayer. I just hold gratitude in my heart for this moment.

Even though everything feels awkward and strange, it also feels nice. Like I belong to something bigger.

Fifteen

"As you can see, the booths are now up and ready to be filled with your beautiful cultures," Ms. Tucker announces through her megaphone as we gather around her in the gym. "Let's make this the best Rainbow Fair ever!"

"Two weeks to go," Katie says as she comes up to me.

"Don't remind me." Anna and I still don't have a clear idea for our booth.

I smile uncertainly at Katie. Things have been a little weird between us this past week. I'm not sure if it's because of the blowup with Allie. Or maybe it's because of Anna. We've been so busy with our different booths that we haven't had a chance to talk other than a few texts and brief exchanges in homeroom.

As if she read my mind, she asks, "Where's Anna?"

"Getting some supplies from her locker. She should be here soon." I pause. "Where are Shane, Megan . . . and Allie?"

"Same. Getting supplies." Her gaze drops, and neither of

us seems to know what to say.

My heart wrenches. I hate this awkwardness between us. "What's going to be in your booth?"

Her face brightens. "You'll see. You should come by and look at it later."

"I will. When we're done, you should come by and look at ours too." It gives me a little burst of joy to say *ours* instead of *mine*.

"Sure," Katie says, but instead of asking any questions about our booth, she bumps my hip with hers. "Hey, we should go hang out today. Allie has a dentist appointment, so we have to finish up in an hour anyway."

A part of me wonders why she assumes I'm free just because it's convenient for her, but most of me is just glad we can finally talk. I miss my best friend.

Then Katie's eyes fix on a spot over my shoulder. "Eek," she whispers.

I whirl around to see Henry and Rowan carrying huge cardboard boxes and bearing down on us with set faces. "Hey, what's up?" she calls out.

"Hi, Katie," Rowan responds, glancing at Henry.

"Hi." Then he sets his box down with a thump, right at my feet. "Sophie, are you going to actually help us today or are you going to abandon us too?" He pointedly doesn't look at

Katie. Wow. Henry has always had strong feelings, but ever since he became a drama kid last year, he's become a bit . . . well, dramatic.

Rowan seems embarrassed and mouths "Sorry" at us both behind Henry's back.

Katie frowns. "I hate to tell you this, Henry, but Sophie isn't in the Chinese booth either."

"Actually . . ." My voice trails off as Katie swivels her gaze to me.

"Give me a minute," I say to Henry and Rowan as I pull Katie aside.

"What's going on, Sophie?" Katie puts her hands on her hips. "Don't tell me that you're trying to do two booths!"

"Shh!" I look around frantically, but it doesn't seem like Ms. Tucker is in sight. "We're not supposed to do more than one booth, remember?"

"Yeah, I remember. I just wasn't sure you did. It's not like you to go around breaking school rules, Sophie."

"I don't have a choice." My voice rises in exasperation, drawing looks from Henry and Rowan. Lowering my voice, I say, "My parents are expecting me to be at the Chinese booth, doing calligraphy in my qípáo."

Katie's eyes widen. "Keeping your parents from finding out you dropped the Chinese booth at Parent-Teacher Night was one thing," she says, "but actually doing the Chinese booth is totally different. How are you going to hide it from Ms. Tucker, and what will you do on the day of the actual Rainbow Fair? Didn't you think this through?"

"Obviously not." The truth is that I was counting on my best friend to help me make this work. I'm clearly making a mess of everything on my own. "Look, the only way Henry and Rowan will let me be a part of their booth is if I help out. So yeah, I'm doing two booths." I catch a glimpse of Ms. Tucker and wait until she's out of sight before adding, "Unofficially, of course."

"Wow, that's a lot." *No kidding.* But at least she doesn't say it in a judgy way.

I give her a hopeful smile. "Any ideas?"

"Sophie, how much longer are you going to be?" Henry asks.

I turn to see Rowan nudge him, and he adds, "I mean, take your time, but I got us some blank scrolls, and you said you've been practicing your calligraphy."

"That's great!" I say, trying to sound enthusiastic.

Another voice calls out cheerfully, "Sorry I'm late, but I've got our stuff!" Anna is balancing two paper bags. She must have just grabbed everything she could from the art supply room.

"Sorry." Katie pats me on the arm. "I have no idea how you're going to pull this off."

"Great," I mumble. There goes my last hope. I take one of the bags from Anna, avoiding Henry's and Rowan's eyes.

Rowan and Henry are talking in low voices, and I can't hear what they're saying, but I can guess. Guilt stabs into me.

"How's the LGBTQ+ booth going?" Anna is asking Katie.

"Hey, Katie," I say quickly. "Why don't you tell Anna about your booth while I talk to Henry and Rowan for a bit."

"I'd love to hear about your booth," Anna says.

"Sure," Katie says to her, but she gives me a look that I can clearly interpret as, *What the heck are you doing?*

Beats me. I walk back to Henry and Rowan.

"Ready to get started?" Rowan's voice is eager.

I guess I have no choice. I have to just come out and say it. "Look, I have three hours before I need to be back home for dinner. I need to help Anna for a couple hours, and then I can give you an hour."

Rowan says, "That sounds goo—"

"Two hours," Henry interrupts. "Since you haven't been pulling your weight with the research part this past week."

He's not wrong. "One and a half hours," I counter.

"One hour and forty-five minutes." Henry has a glint in his

eyes like he's gotten a taste for making deals. I'll bet this kid is no stranger to the bargaining world of Chinese night markets.

"One and a half hours, and I'll throw in a box of egg tarts. Last offer." Henry isn't the only one who's been to a night market. My parents took me to one when we visited Taiwan last summer.

"Deal." Henry and I shake hands.

"Deal," Rowan echoes, looking at the bag on my shoulder as if I'm going to whip out the egg tarts right then and there.

"I'll bring them tomorrow," I promise, walking back to Anna and Katie with relief. Anna is so easygoing that I'm sure she won't mind splitting the booth prep time with Henry and Rowan.

"Katie's booth sounds amazing!" Anna says to me as I reach them.

Katie smiles. "Thanks."

It makes me feel happy to see my two friends get along. Maybe the three of us can all be friends.

Voices float toward us, and without turning around, I can tell who it is. My back stiffens, and I have to remind myself that they're my friends too. Sort of.

"Should we have gotten more glitter glue?" That would be Megan.

"We have more than enough!" Allie, of course.

"Is there such a thing as too much glitter glue?" And that's Shane.

I'm good with Shane and Megan, but I haven't seen Allie since last week's awkward encounter, and I'm still not sure what to think of that.

Quickly, Katie says, "Sophie, so we're on to hang out in about an hour? It's been forever."

Oh no. I totally forgot that she'd asked me to hang out. The thing making my chest tight now isn't Allie. It's having to let Katie down.

She must see my answer on my face because her eyes harden. "Let me guess. You can't because you're working on the Muslim booth. Again."

That is so unfair. Sudden anger spurts into me. "I'm not the only one with a new booth, and we didn't hang out this past week because we were *both* busy with Rainbow Fair prep."

Anna's eyes dart between us. "Sophie, I'm fine with finishing up in an hour so you can hang out with Katie."

"I can't." I meet Katie's eyes. "I promised Henry and Rowan I'd help with the Chinese booth since they're down to just the two of them."

"Am I supposed to feel bad because I'm not helping too?"

Katie's voice is rising. "Because it's your choice to lie to your parents."

I gape at her, not knowing what to say, because Katie has always been on my side. A hot mass rises in my chest.

Her eyes drop, and she flushes like she knows she's gone too far.

"Is this a bad time?" Megan asks as she, Allie, and Shane come up to us.

"No," Katie mutters. "Let's get started on our booth."

"Anna and I need to work on our booth too." I unlock my frozen legs and move to stand next to her. "Did you know that Muslims are one of the most diverse communities? Many different cultures practice Islam." Okay, that was a little random, but I want Katie to know her booth isn't the only cool one. I'm still upset that she expects me to support her booth when she hasn't shown any interest in mine.

But my anger fades when Katie doesn't say anything, her face still and hard. There's never been tension between us before, and I don't know how to handle it. Heaviness drags at my heart.

"Yeah, that's right." Anna says, her eyes uncertain. "Muslims are very diverse." What must she be thinking of all this?

"Cool," Shane says, their voice determinedly bright. They

turn to Anna. "It's nice to meet you. I'm Shane, and my pronouns are they/them."

"It's nice to meet you too, Shane." She smiles. "I'm Anna. She/her pronouns."

Allie's eyebrows rise, and I wonder if she's surprised about Anna accepting Shane's gender nonbinary pronouns so easily. "I'm Allie," she says. "She/her pronouns." She's not looking at me at all, but maybe she's just embarrassed about last week.

"Hi, Anna," Megan says. "I'm Megan, and my pronouns are she/her too."

"Remember that we only have an hour to set up our booth today," Allie says. "I have that dentist appointment."

"I guess we'll get started, then," Megan says awkwardly. She hesitates and adds, "Sophie, our next LGBTQ+ Student Union meeting is open to allies, and it would be great if you can come."

"Oh." My eyes go to Katie. Does she even want me there? "Thanks. Um, I'll see if I can make it."

Katie doesn't meet my eyes or respond.

Shane glances at Katie and then smiles at me. "Good. We'll see you there, Sophie."

There's a sick feeling in my stomach. Things are far from normal between Katie and me.

"Anna, you're welcome too," Shane says. "Sophie can tell you all about it."

"Sounds great," Anna says, but she's peering at me worriedly.

I stare after them as they leave, watching Katie's stiff back as she walks away, willing her to turn around and smile or give me some sign that it will be okay between us.

But Katie doesn't turn around.

Sixteen

Anna sets her bag on the table of our booth. Everyone starts out with a folding table, but we're supposed to use butcher paper and markers to transform it into something that looks like a fair booth. "What was that about?" she asks.

I put the bag I'm carrying next to hers. "It's complicated." How do I explain how an eight-year friendship exploded when I don't understand it myself? Tears sting my eyes.

Anna just looks at me with that open, sympathetic expression, and before I know, I'm telling her everything. The Chinese booth. Lying to my parents. Not telling Katie I'm Muslim. The fight with Allie. My fear that Katie is leaving me for her other friends. My anger that she seems to resent my new friendship with Anna.

"Wow," Anna says when I'm done. "You're right. That does sound complicated."

"Yeah." I stare at the bare wood of the booth, trying to imagine what it will look like by the time Rainbow Fair happens in two weeks. I just can't imagine it. Will Katie and I even be on speaking terms then?

"But it sounds like you and Katie have been good friends for a long time. I'm sure you'll get through this."

I think of the slideshow I made of our friendship to convince my parents to let me go to Katie's birthday party and all the times we've had each other's backs. "At least she stood up to Allie for me." But then she walked away without a word to me after our fight just now. I frown and then blurt out the fear gnawing at me. "I'm worried that things are weird between us because some part of Katie believes what Allie said."

"Oh, I don't think so. Like you said, Katie probably just feels left out."

Her sureness eases my anxiety, but there's still an ache in my heart. "I think she's mad that I didn't tell her I'm Muslim, but it's not like it was supposed to be a secret."

"Totally," she says evenly, "but can I ask you why you didn't tell Katie you are Muslim?" There's no judgment in Anna's voice. She just sounds curious.

Anna already knows my family doesn't practice much, but it still feels weird to talk about my confusion about being Muslim. The words stick in my throat, but I push them out. "I didn't really know if I was Muslim even though my parents kept telling me I was. It's not like we went to a mosque or prayed, so I didn't know what it meant for me to be Muslim. I *still* don't know. I guess it was just easier not to talk about it, especially since I already felt different enough being Chinese."

I think of the kid in second grade who asked if Chinese people ate dogs and the kid who called Katie and me "Chinese virus." It would have been so much worse if I didn't have Katie as my best friend.

Anna nods encouragingly, and the words come more easily now. "Katie always understood how horrible it was to be seen as weird just because we're Chinese. But I didn't know how to talk to her about being Muslim."

My stomach knots as I remember Allie asking me how I can be Muslim and still be friends with them when Muslims kill gays. There are a million things I wish I said to her. If I could do it all over again, I'd tell her that Islam is a religion of peace and that it wasn't fair for her to think that all Muslims are violent and homophobic. But I wasn't used to people assuming I was an awful person because of my religion. Maybe I wasn't exactly hiding being Muslim, but there was a reason I didn't talk about it. And I can see why Katie was angry that I didn't tell her. It must have seemed like I didn't trust her.

But it wasn't that. "Katie is my best friend. I didn't want her, of all people, to see me as different."

"I understand." Anna's eyes are sympathetic.

Having someone listen and really *get* it is calming me down. I can even give Allie the benefit of the doubt. "I suppose it's not like Allie said anything really terrible."

A shadow crosses Anna's face. "She didn't call you a terrorist, at least."

My jaw drops. "Did someone call you that? Just because you're Muslim?"

She nods. "It was at my old school." No wonder she thinks everyone is so nice here at Monroe.

"Allie wouldn't ever do that." Then I think about it. Just because Allie didn't call me a terrorist, it doesn't mean that no one ever would. If I keep telling people I'm Muslim, maybe someone will think I'm a terrorist too. Is that why my parents tell people we don't eat pork for "cultural reasons" instead of saying we're Muslim? Because it can be dangerous for people to know we're Muslim? Sadness fills me.

"It still wasn't okay for Allie to make assumptions about you just because you're Muslim," Anna says.

"You're right." It's icky knowing people might treat me differently because I'm Muslim, but my body still feels as if a big, messy knot has been pulled loose inside me. I didn't know what a relief it would be to talk to someone about this stuff. In the interest of fairness, I add, "Katie did say Allie is sorry. Maybe she is. And I can sort of understand where Allie was coming from too. Some people do use their religion in really awful ways."

"Yes, but not just Muslims."

"That's a good point." I think about how some Christian conservatives use *their* religion. "Like the people trying to ban books and pass anti-trans laws in schools."

"True." Anna starts unpacking one of the bags. "I'm sorry things are so rough between you and Katie right now. I went through something like this last year with my best friend."

"Really? What happened?" I hope her story has a happy ending.

"Nora was Muslim like me, and we got used to doing everything together and thinking the same way." *Like Katie and me.* Anna pulls out sheets of paper and markers. "It wasn't easy at our school, and I think it was worse for Nora. She chose to start wearing a hijab, and she got teased for it."

"That's awful." I start unpacking the second bag and yank out a box of pushpins with unnecessary force, taking out my feelings on the supplies.

"Yes, it was." She pauses. "Nora could handle the teasing, but it was even worse when our friends treated her like she was being oppressed or something. I haven't decided whether I'm going to wear a hijab, but if I do, it will be my choice and not something I was forced to do by my religion."

"I get that." I'm not sure where Anna's story is going, but a lump is already forming in my throat.

"Anyway, there were a whole bunch of things like that. We couldn't always get excused from class to pray, and even if we did, there wasn't a place to pray."

"Oh. There isn't a place to pray at Monroe either, is there?"

"No," she says simply. "I just pray when and where I can."

It's times like these when I feel like a bad Muslim. How could I have not realized that there wasn't a prayer space sooner? "Sorry," I mumble.

"Don't be." Anna smiles. "Remember I told you there's more than one way to be Muslim? That goes for prayer too. Nora and I didn't pray the same way, but we respected those differences."

"What happened then?"

Her smile fades. "Nora got fed up with being disrespected for her faith and beliefs. I mean, we both were, but . . ." Anna takes a deep breath. "What Nora did wasn't right, but she was hurting."

I have a feeling the happy ending I'm hoping for isn't coming. "What did your friend do?"

"There was a trans girl at our school, and we didn't have any gender-neutral bathrooms or locker rooms."

Oh no. My throat goes hot and dry. I do *not* like where this is going.

Anna bites her lip. "Nora said that Islam didn't allow for her to share a locker room with boys."

That's what I was afraid of. "So your friend misgendered someone and made her feel unsafe." Oops. I didn't mean to sound so harsh, but I couldn't keep the anger out of my voice.

"Pretty much." Anna shakes her head. "Shannon wasn't even using the girls' locker room. She was changing in the staff bathroom before PE. I told Nora that what she was doing was just as bad as anything that was done to us, but she wouldn't listen. Anyway, our friendship was never the same."

I'm silent, my hands frozen on whatever I just pulled from the bag. Things might suck between Katie and me right now, but at least it's not as terrible as what happened between Anna and her friend. "It sounds like they actually had something in common."

Anna looks at me with a puzzled frown. "What do you mean?"

"Well, your friend Nora didn't have a place to pray and didn't feel like her religious identity was being respected. Shannon didn't have a gender-neutral bathroom or locker room to use, and I'm sure she didn't feel like her gender identity was being respected."

"Yes, you're right."

"It's too bad they couldn't work together to get what they

both needed." My heart hurts as I think about Katie trying to get better alternative lunches and me signing the petition for an LGBTQ+ booth. I need to talk to Katie. I just wish I knew how.

Anna is looking at the assortment of construction paper and markers we have spread out on the counter of our booth. "What are we going to do with all this?"

"I'm not sure. I think Ms. Tucker was expecting us to hang up prayer rugs and display Arabian lanterns or something."

She laughs. "People don't realize that Islam isn't just one culture."

An idea starts bubbling up in me. *There's more than one way to be Muslim.* "What if," I say slowly, "we use our booth to show people that? We could focus on all the different ways of being Muslim and how Islam has been misunderstood."

Anna's eyes light up. "Like what wearing a hijab would mean to me?"

"Yes! And like how I'm Hui, and no one has even heard of us."

"And all the other cultures too," she adds. "Black Muslims. South Asian Muslims. We can show how diverse we are."

I'm looking at our empty booth, seeing it come alive. "And I'm sure there are Muslims who are also LGBTQ+ too. We could have their stories here."

"I love that."

We stare at each other, my own excitement reflected in Anna's face.

This is going to be the *best* Rainbow Fair booth ever.

Seventeen

This is going to be the *worst* Rainbow Fair booth ever.

I stare at the blob of black ink I accidentally dripped over the Tang dynasty poem I'm copying on rice paper. I put my brush down on the newspaper we have spread over our table and sigh. I've only been here five minutes, and I'm already messing up.

Luckily, Henry is copying Confucian sayings on his own rice paper and doesn't seem to notice. Rowan, who's putting up red cut-outs of Chinese characters on the wall behind our table, doesn't seem to notice either. *Wait a second.*

I peer closer at the characters she's hanging up with blue painters tape. "Rowan, I think the double-happiness character is supposed to be used just for weddings."

"I know," she says, "but Henry said no one else will know."

"Our parents will know," I point out, "and they're all coming to look at our booth at Rainbow Fair." Which is why I'm here, making a mess of my Chinese calligraphy.

"Good point." She sets down the red cut-outs and blue tape.

Henry looks up from his calligraphy. "Okay, take down the double-happiness characters. We can hang up some red lanterns instead." He glances at my paper and frowns. "What happened here?"

"I messed up," I say, stating the obvious.

"You can just cut off the top part," he suggests. "The rest of it looks okay."

"I'm not going to randomly cut out part of the poem. And before you say no one will notice, I'm going to remind you, once again, that our parents will be able to tell if there's a huge chunk missing." I gesture at the ink spreading over the top half of the paper. "Chinese writing goes left to right, not top to bottom, remember? If I cut off the top part, it won't make sense."

"Fine. You can start over, but try not to mess up again. We don't have much rice paper."

I peer over at his blocky writing. My calligraphy isn't great, but it's certainly better than his. He doesn't even seem to be paying attention to the stroke order of the characters and is just randomly copying the printout he has in front of him. "What does that even say?"

"No clue."

I glance at my ruined Tang dynasty poem. "Yeah, me neither."

"Oh no." Henry has just ripped the thin rice paper with an aggressive stroke of his brush. "I guess I'll have to start over too."

Rowan pauses in peeling blue painter's tape off the backs of the double-happiness characters. "We can use some of this tape to fix your scroll." She comes over to stick a piece of tape to the back of the scroll. It does hold it together, but the paper is so thin that the blue tape is visible. She examines the scroll, and her face falls. "Robots are so much easier to fix."

I blink. "Um, that's going to need some explanation."

"I meant that when a robot isn't working right, I just need to fix the code." She tries to smooth out the taped-up scroll. "I'm in the robotics club."

"Got it." I set aside my own scroll to put in the recycling bin and make a mental note to check if ink-soaked rice paper can be recycled. "Too bad you can't build us a robot for our booth."

"I wish." She sighs. "The other kids in the robotics club wanted to do that for their booth, but Ms. Tucker wouldn't let them."

Huh? "There's a robot booth at Rainbow Fair?"

Rowan shakes her head. "No. It's just that the rest of the club all signed up for the Norwegian booth so they could be together. I'm not even sure if they're all Norwegian, but who's going to check?" Her face falls. "That wouldn't work for me. Obviously."

Of course. Anger rises up in me. "It's not fair that they're leaving you out."

"Oh, I'm used to it." Her voice is fake-cheerful. "I'm the only girl too, but I don't think the boys mean to leave me out."

"It still isn't fair." Henry slams his brush down so it splashes black ink on the newspaper-covered counter. "It's like how I'm the only Asian in drama and always have to be an extra."

Katie would be up in arms over this. My breath shortens at the thought of her. She would know what to do, but she's not here. Maybe it's time for me to step up and see what I can do without her.

I look at Henry with his ink-smeared face and Rowan with her vain attempts with the blue tape. Their talents are totally wasted.

I remember what Anna said. *There's more than one way to be Muslim.*

Why can't there be more than one way to be Chinese too?

Excitement bubbles in me as I say to Henry and Rowan, "I have an idea for our booth. Rowan, Ms. Tucker wouldn't approve of a robot, but do you think you can tie your robotics stuff into the Chinese booth?"

Rowan's eyes shine, and she answers at once. "Ooh! I could do Asian mech drawings for the booth."

I have no idea what that means, but it sounds good to me. "Great. And, Henry, is there a Chinese play or something that you can use for our booth?"

"I don't really know Chinese plays that well."

"Maybe you can do some research?" And speaking of research, I can totally use what I'm learning about Hui history and culture in the Chinese booth. This can be a win-win.

"I could." He doesn't sound enthusiastic.

Maybe I should let Henry decide what he wants to do. "What are your ideas?"

"Well . . ." He pauses and looks like he's thinking. "I've always wanted to act in a Shakespeare play set in ancient China."

Not what I was expecting, but who am I to judge? "Sure! That sounds great."

"I love that idea, Henry." Rowan is rummaging in a box. "Do we have anything other than rice paper? I need thicker paper for my mech drawings."

"Yeah, I think I grabbed some." Henry helps her look. "If I do *Hamlet*, which dynasty do you think would be better? Song or Qing?"

I smile. It looks like my boothmates are off and running. But something about this doesn't seem quite right. A pang hits my heart when I realize what's missing.

My best friend. I need Katie.

Eighteen

Hey Katie, I type.

No. That sounds too casual, like I'm ignoring the fact that we haven't talked or texted since our fight on Friday. My heart twists. I tried to text Katie over the weekend, but I just didn't know what to say. Now we're in class before the first bell on Monday morning, and it's ridiculous that I'm texting her when she's just three desks away. My gaze goes to where Katie is sitting, and of course she's not looking at me. She's deep in conversation with Megan, who's sitting next to her. A pang of sadness shoots through me. The desk on the other side of Katie, where I usually sit, is empty. Instead, I'm sitting in the back row because I couldn't bear being so close to her when she's practically giving me the silent treatment.

Ms. Tucker is still at her computer and won't make us put our phones away until the first bell has rung. I delete the draft of my text and try again.

Dear Katie.

Ugh. That sounds way too formal, like I'm writing to a pen pal I barely know instead of my best friend since kindergarten.

Katie, we need to talk.

Isn't that the start to every breakup text? I bite my lip. I definitely don't want to sound like I'm ending our friendship.

What's up? Long time no talk.

Nope. Just nope. "Argghh," I groan.

"What's wrong?" a voice asks.

I look up from my phone to find Lucas, the kid with the cool idea for the Black culture booth, peering at me from the desk next to mine.

"It's nothing." I flush and put my phone away.

He glances over at Ms. Tucker and then back at me. Lowering his voice, he asks, "Is it the Muslim booth? Because it wasn't okay how Ms. Tucker pressured you into doing it."

"Oh." I stare at my feet. It's sweet of Lucas to be concerned, but I can't let him think I resent doing the Muslim booth. "Actually, that's turning out kind of great."

"Really?"

I nod and add, "I mean, I don't love how it happened." By that, I mean Katie accidentally outing me as Muslim and Ms. Tucker plopping me into the Muslim booth without asking me first, but even those things don't matter that much. What really bothers me is that I had to give up the Chinese booth. "I'm learning a lot, and working with Anna is awesome." I hesitate. "I just wish I could do the Chinese one too."

"Yeah. These rules make no sense."

Lucas is probably thinking about Ms. Tucker's suggestion that he focus on African culture for the Black culture booth. I clear my throat. "I'm sorry for not saying anything when Ms. Tucker tried to tell you what to do for your booth. I think your display of books by Black authors is really cool."

"Thanks." Lucas grimaces. "Ms. Tucker's rules for Rainbow Fair are the worst."

"They really are."

We share a conspiratorial grin, and then he says, "Listen, if you know of any Black Muslim authors, I could display their books in our booth."

I smile and unzip my backpack. "Actually, Anna just lent me some books to read, and this one is by a Black Muslim author. I'm loving it so far." I hand him my copy of Autumn Allen's *All You Have to Do*.

"This looks great," he says, reading the jacket description. "Were you planning to use it for your booth?"

That's exactly what Anna and I were planning. "It's just a

few books, not the whole booth like yours." Unease flutters in my stomach. "Is that okay? I don't want to copy your idea."

Lucas laughs, handing me back the book. "It's not like we copyrighted the idea to have books in our booth. I was just asking because I thought it would be cool for both booths to display the book. Maybe on our description card, we can say something like 'Check out the Muslim booth for more information.'"

"I love that idea! Our description can say, 'Check out the Black culture booth for more information.'" Ms. Tucker might be able to keep us from being in more than one booth, but she can't stop us from making connections like this.

"Sounds like a plan. Hey, do you think Katie would want to do the same thing with the LGBTQ+ booth and have a joint display of an LGBTQ Black author?"

My body stiffens. For a moment, I had forgotten about the weirdness with Katie, and now all my sadness comes crashing down on me again. "I'm sure she'd love to," I reply woodenly.

Lucas frowns and looks over at Katie, who's still talking to Megan with her back turned to me. Sympathy spreads over his face. "Don't tell me you and Katie are fighting."

We'd have to be talking to be fighting, and we're definitely not talking. "Not exactly," I hedge, and I *want* it to be true. I hope it's true.

If we *are* in a fight, then I'm not entirely sure what we're fighting about.

"Are you sure this is okay?" I ask Anna as I nervously smooth down my shirt over my skirt and leggings.

When Anna suggested that we go to her mosque's annual neighborhood barbecue, I agreed immediately, but now I'm having second thoughts. Even though she said it was a casual event, my outfit feels too informal for a mosque.

"Yes, you look fine." She smiles at me. "Ready?"

Not really, but at least we're going on a day when the mosque, or at least its parking lot, is open to everyone. Even though I am Muslim, I don't feel comfortable enough in my knowledge of Islamic practice to go at a time of regular prayers.

"Shouldn't we wait for your parents?" They had dropped us off near the mosque while they went to look for parking.

"No, let's go ahead. They'll meet us as soon as they park."

"Okay then." I hide my anxiety and let her lead me toward the mosque. I've done my research and know that this mosque, tucked into a neighborhood in North Seattle, is built in an arabesque style. Still, I'm not prepared for the catch in my throat as we approach the mosque with its green dome (which I've learned is called a qubba) and the slim tower (which I've learned is called a minaret) with its crescent moon spire.

It's beautiful.

The frantic beat of my heart begins to steady as we walk around the side of the building to where the barbecue is being held. White awnings dot the concrete lot, and a big banner with red letters proclaims, "Annual Neighborhood Gathering."

People are filling their plates with food, and the delicious smells coming from the grills behind the long tables make my stomach rumble. At least I know there won't be pork at this barbecue. My parents would love it.

Guilt creeps into me. They would probably think it was great that I was learning more about Islam, but I'm trying to keep Anna and my parents apart because my new friend is incapable of deception and would probably spill everything about the Muslim booth within five minutes of meeting my parents. Then they would know I'm not doing the Chinese booth . . . and cue the disappointment.

So, instead, I told my parents I was working on the Chinese booth today and had them drop me off at the library. As if that wasn't bad enough, there was a look of disappointment on Anna's face when I asked her to pick me up from the library instead of my house. Not only did I lie to my parents, but I also kept my new friend a secret from them and made her feel bad about it. Basically, I'm kind of a terrible daughter and friend right now. No doubt Katie would agree.

Shoving away thoughts of Katie, I whisper to Anna, "There are so many people here. Are they from your mosque or the neighborhood?"

"Mostly people from my mosque, but I hear some locals always come."

I peer around the parking lot, bright with people talking and laughing. I was just trying to sound cool when I told Katie that Islam was one of the most diverse religions, but now that I'm here, I can see how true that statement actually was. Seattle, especially North Seattle, is pretty white, but you'd never know it looking around this barbecue.

So this is where all the BIPOC people in North Seattle are. Katie would love it here too.

"What's wrong?" Anna asks me as we join a line for food.

"Sorry." I smile and try to shake off my sadness. "I was wishing Katie could see this." She's always talking about how she wished Rainbow Fair could be like the family-friendly Pride Festival that happens every year at Volunteer Park. I want to tell her about this barbecue at a mosque that reminds me of the Pride Festival.

"You still haven't talked to her?"

I'm saved from answering when a woman in a hijab turns around to Anna. "Assalamu alaikum."

"Wa alaikum as-salam," Anna replies.

I tense up. There's no way I can pronounce the "And peace be upon you too" return greeting. Then I remember that there are non-Muslims here too, so everyone will assume that I'm not Muslim if I don't return the greeting. My body relaxes.

"I remember seeing you at the mosque," the woman says to Anna in a friendly tone. "You and your parents are new here, aren't you?"

"Yes. We just moved here from California." Anna gestures to me. "This is my friend Sophie. She's Muslim too."

I gulp. So much for flying under the radar.

The woman smiles at me. "Assalamu alaikum."

Heat rushes to my face. "I'm just starting to learn about Islam," I say shyly.

The woman's smile doesn't waver. She doesn't seem to be questioning how it is that I'm Muslim but don't speak the most basic Arabic to greet other Muslims. "It's wonderful that you came to our barbecue today. I made the pasta salad over there," she says, pointing to a bright blue bowl at the end of the table. "Make sure you try it."

I blink in surprise at her easy acceptance. "I will. Thanks."

A boy and a girl come running up to the woman, trailed by their father, and more greetings are exchanged. Anna squeezes my hand, and this time, I don't feel as self-conscious about not returning the greetings. Maybe I'll be able to speak these Islamic phrases in Arabic one day, but it's okay if I'm not ready yet.

Anna and I fill our plates with meat and vegetable kebabs, corn on the cob, pasta salad (of course), and various sweets. As we carry our food over to the tables under the awnings, I notice an informational booth about the mosque along with booths that have art supplies and bottles of bubbles for the younger kids to play with. Everyone seems to be having a great time.

"This is what Rainbow Fair should be like," I say. "I wish our whole school could see how many different kinds of Muslims there are." Then an idea hits me. "Hey, do you think we can take pictures?"

Anna's face lights up. "Of course. Are you thinking of putting up pictures in our booth?"

"I have an even better idea." In my mind, I can see images of the barbecue, clips from videos like the one Anna showed me of hajj (because she dreams of making the annual pilgrimage to Mecca one day), clips I showed Anna from the *Ms. Marvel* show (because I think I might be starting to love Kamala Khan, Pakistani Muslim superhero, even more than Wonder Woman), images of the *Ms. Marvel* comics, and passages from books by Muslim authors. "I'm thinking of a slideshow."

"I love that!"

"We can set up my laptop in the booth and just keep the slideshow running. I did one about recycling I can show you." Then I remember my last slideshow, the one talking my parents into letting me go to Katie's sleepover. "Katie—" My breath goes short, and I can't finish whatever it was that I was going to say. I miss Katie so much.

Anna's expression is sympathetic. "You never did tell me whether you talked to Katie."

"I want to . . ." My voice trails off. "You know how I told you about the Muslim and the Black culture booths connecting our booths with a common book?"

She nods, but her eyes are puzzled, like she's not sure where I'm going with this.

"Lucas asked me if I thought Katie would be interested in doing the same thing with the LGBTQ+ booth, and I just froze," I say. "Knowing Katie, she already has a couple of queer rom-coms by Black authors. I could have offered to check with Katie, and it would have been the perfect excuse to talk to her, but I blew it."

A pang hits me as I think of the signed copy of *Not Your Sidekick* that I gave Katie for her birthday. She had it displayed prominently on her bookshelf, but it might be dumped into a box and shoved to the back of her closet at this point.

"Do you really need an excuse to talk to her?" Anna asks.

"Apparently, I do." I think of the many, many deleted drafts of texts to her. "It's been three days since we last talked, and now I don't even know where to begin."

Anna is silent for a moment, but then a slow smile spreads over her face. "I think I have an idea."

Nineteen

I swing my backpack over my shoulder like I'm going on an epic quest instead of making the walk from the Muslim booth to the LGBTQ+ booth.

"You've got this." Anna gives me a thumbs-up.

"Thanks." My smile is wobbly. "Here I go." But my feet stay rooted to the ground.

Anna comes around the folding table, points me in the direction of the LGBTQ+ booth, and gives me a friendly little shove. "Go, then."

Reluctantly, I start walking. The problem is that I don't know if Katie is still there. It's been over an hour since school ended, and she and the others might be done working on their booth for the day. If I hadn't been such a coward, I would have gone earlier, but the truth is that I'm afraid. It will be devastating if Katie rejects me. Then we really won't be friends anymore. Sweat prickles at my neck.

All around me are kids putting up handmade posters, but I

don't see Katie until I get to the far corner of the gym. There's a huge, glittery rainbow hanging behind the table. Despite Allie's objection, it looks like there wasn't too much glitter glue after all.

My breath catches when I spot Katie. She's bent over something at the table, and she's alone. My steps slow as I approach. What if she's still mad and won't want to talk to me?

Too bad. We need to get past this, and that means talking to each other.

My heartbeat races as I quicken my pace.

She looks up, and for a moment, she looks happy to see me, but then her face clouds over. "What are you doing here, Sophie?" She sounds wary as she sets down a pink marker and picks up a purple one.

My tongue thickens, and I don't know how to answer her. Then I remember what's in my backpack. Out of the corner of my eye, I see Leah Johnson's book *You Should See Me in a Crown* on the table, and the card Katie is working on says, "For more information, see the Black culture booth." Good. It looks like Lucas already got to her.

I take off my backpack, set it on her table, and unzip it. "I have something for you. Actually, it's Anna's idea."

Her face is unreadable, and my hands shake as I thrust

the book at her. "Here. Anna has two copies of the book, and we thought we'd display one copy at the Muslim booth, and maybe you could display another at the LGBTQ+ booth? It's a young adult rom-com because I know you love those."

Katie stares down at *Hani and Ishu's Guide to Fake Dating* by Adiba Jaigirdar. Slowly, she looks back up at me. "Are you sure you want to work with another booth? I thought you were already working on two booths."

"I am." I swallow past the lump of nerves in my throat. "But I realized something."

"What's that?"

Now or never. I take a deep breath. "I can't do this without my best friend."

For a long moment, Katie doesn't say anything, and my heart beats so loudly that I wonder if she can hear it.

At last she breaks the silence. "Are you sure I'm still your best friend?"

My heart falls with a painful thud. This can't be how our friendship ends.

"Because I've been a horrible friend lately," she adds, her voice sounding clogged.

Relief and hope fill my chest. "Me too," I admit. "But I miss you."

"I miss you too." A sad look comes over her face. "Do you

remember when Ms. Tucker put you in charge of the Muslim booth?"

"How could I forget?" Even now, my hands go clammy at the memory. "I hadn't told anyone I was Muslim. Not even you."

"And then you *did* tell me, and I outed you."

"It was an accident," I say quickly. "It wasn't your fault that Ms. Tucker overheard."

"I know, but I should have been more careful, and I'm sorry about that." I open my mouth, but she waves off my protest. "Anyway, that's not what I'm trying to say. The thing is that you came out as Muslim before you were ready, and then Ms. Tucker asked you to run a Muslim booth all by yourself." She's getting at something, but I'm not sure what it is.

"What made you do it?" Katie asks. She asked me before, but this seems different. She doesn't seem to be questioning my decision this time.

"I'm not sure. It was the scariest thing I've ever done." I remember the fear that shook me to the core in that moment. "I wasn't sure if I even had the right to say I was Muslim. I mean, my family doesn't really practice. I was afraid that if I did the booth, everyone would see me as a fraud."

She nods. "I get that. It's like I wasn't sure if I could say I was queer because I like boys too." *Yes, Katie would have understood.* "But I had you and Shane, Allie, and Megan to talk to, and you all supported me. You didn't have anyone to talk to." Her voice drops. "I wish you had told me earlier. I would have been there for you."

Heat builds up in the back of my eyes. "I wish I had told you too. I'm sorry I didn't."

"Why didn't you?" Katie bites her lip. "Is it because you didn't trust me?"

"No!" This is what I was afraid of. "I can see why you would think that, but it was never about not trusting you." She doesn't look convinced, and my stomach knots. How do I explain? Then I remember what Katie told me when she first came out as bisexual. I was the first person she told, even before she told her parents. "Do you remember what you said to me when you first came out to me as bi?"

Katie's face eases out of its tense lines. "I told you that I was just starting to figure out that I was bi."

"It was the same with me. I just . . . hadn't figured out things yet. I mean, I know it's different because my parents knew I was Muslim. The point is that I wasn't trying to keep secrets. It just didn't seem like a big part of my life before. Not until the Muslim booth."

"I can relate to that." Her mouth quirks up in a wry smile. "Can I ask you another question, then?"

I nod, still too clogged with emotion to speak.

"Even when you thought you had to do the Muslim booth on your own, why did you say yes?"

"Because," I say slowly. "It felt scarier to say no. To lose what I didn't even know I wanted. So it didn't feel brave at the time. It just felt like what I had to do. How other people thought I should be or how Muslims should be—I didn't want to let all that stop me from being who I am."

"Good. Because who you are is awesome." Katie puts the book I gave her on one of the two empty stands next to the Leah Johnson book. Then she takes another book out of a box on the table and sets it up on the other stand. It's the signed copy of *Not Your Sidekick*, the book I gave her for her birthday. "And you're the most amazing friend too."

Katie rushes around the table. And then we're hugging each other and sniffling in each other's arms.

Eventually, I pull away, wiping my eyes. "I'm sorry I didn't make time for you."

"I'm sorry I was so mean about it." Katie blinks tears from her eyes. "You were spending all this time with Anna, and I started to wonder if I was being replaced."

"Never." My chest constricts, and I'm not sure if I should say this part, but if we're going to get past this, then we need to be honest with each other. "I kind of felt the same way when you started hanging out with Megan, Allie, and Shane."

"I know." She stares at her feet before looking up again. "You're my best friend, Sophie. Nothing is going to change that."

Tears sting the back of my eyes. "You're my best friend too." Maybe things will change again next year when we're in eighth grade or when we start high school, but in my heart, I'm certain that nothing can take away what we are right now to each other.

"And I'm sorry I said you were lying to your parents," she adds.

"But I am. Lying to my parents, I mean." I feel sick to my stomach saying it out loud.

"I still shouldn't have said that. Some LGBTQ+ kids at school aren't out to their parents, and I would never say they're being dishonest."

"This is different." I have to think it over before I can explain why. "I'm not trying to hide being Muslim from my *parents*, of all people. They're proud about being Muslim." I hesitate as I think of how they give "cultural reasons" as an excuse for not eating pork. "Maybe it's more complicated than that, but if they keep quiet about being Muslim, it's because people have some messed-up ideas about us. My parents aren't *ashamed* of being Muslim. And they're proud of being Chinese too. I just don't want them to feel I'm not proud that I'm Chinese."

"Yeah, that makes sense." Katie is looking at me as if she really does understand. "I mean, my parents are super supportive of me being bi, but they want me to be as proud of being Chinese as I am of being bi. They're disappointed I'm giving up the Chinese booth, actually."

Yeah, I kind of picked up on that at the Parent-Teacher Curriculum Night.

Katie walks back over to the booth, and I follow her. "See this poster?"

It looks like she's making a gender unicorn poster with gender and gender-identity terms written in sparkly pink and purple. "It looks awesome." I still don't get what it has to do with her parents.

"Thanks. We want to make these ideas clear, not just to other kids, but the parents coming by the booth." She traces the black outline of the unicorn, which hasn't been colored in yet. "While I was working on this, the others started saying how cool and understanding my parents are." She doesn't sound happy about this, and I'm not sure why. Her parents *are* awesome.

"The point is they made it sound like my parents were different," she continues. "Not like most Asian parents."

"Oh." I understand now. It's kind of like our counselor wondering if my parents were pressuring me. And like Ms. Terrence, it's not like Katie's friends were doing anything wrong. It just stinks to fight against a stereotype all the time.

Katie looks back up at me. "I lashed out at you before because I felt guilty. I wanted to help with the Chinese booth like you, but I was afraid the others would think I'm being pressured into it by my parents."

"It's not that simple, is it?" I can totally relate.

"No, it isn't. Like I said, my parents are super supportive, but they don't get why I can't be both bi *and* Chinese."

"Why can't you?" The question pops out before I can help it. "I mean, it's the Rainbow Fair that's making you choose between booths. It's not like you *actually* have to choose between being bi and Chinese." I stop and listen to my own words. "Just like I don't have to choose between being Muslim and Chinese."

Katie nods. "You're right, but I don't know what to do about it. Look at you, being pulled between two booths." She doesn't sound critical, just sympathetic.

"Yeah, that's not working out so great for me." I glance at

her. "I have an idea that will change everything, but we have to keep it quiet."

Her eyebrows shoot up. "Sophie Hu, straight-A student and incurable rule-follower, are you actually trying to lead me into trouble?"

Yes. Absolutely. "It may or may not be just a *little* bit against the rules."

A smile spreads over her face. "I am so in."

Twenty

"Does anyone have a skull?" Henry asks.

It's a week later, and Katie and I are helping Henry and Rowan at the Chinese booth.

Katie gapes at him, and I explain, "It's for his *Hamlet* performance." How Henry was able to write a whole one-person play in just one week is beyond me. Now all he has to do is memorize the lines in the week before Rainbow Fair.

"Oh right," she says. "Sorry, no skull."

Rowan shakes her head. "Me neither." She starts looking in the box of props Henry borrowed from the theater. "Isn't there one here?"

"You'd think." He sighs and adjusts the robe of his Chinese warrior costume. This is the first time he's practicing his lines in full costume and accompanied by Chinese opera on Bluetooth speakers.

I point to his helmet. "Didn't you bring an extra helmet?" He'd brought a box of props from home today in addition to the ones he got from the school theater.

He brightens. "Yes, and that's perfect, actually. In my script, Hamlet is talking to the skull of his dead warrior friend."

I grab the helmet from his box, and as I hand it to him, the alarm on my phone goes off.

I turn off the alarm. "That's our cue." Ms. Tucker checks up on every booth around this time every day, and Katie and I always make sure to be at our assigned booth when she makes her rounds. There are other adults who are supposed to be supervising the Rainbow Fair preparations, but Ms. Tucker is the only adult keeping track of who's supposed to be in which booth.

I'm just about to step around the table when I spot Ms. Tucker coming into the gym.

My heart goes haywire. "Oh no! She's early!" Grabbing Katie's arm, I pull her down to crouch next to me behind the Chinese booth. Red butcher paper hangs down from all sides of the table, hiding us from sight. "Henry, start your speech," I whisper urgently. "Rowan, cover up Katie's Mandarin gender unicorn poster and the card for the book." The book is *Not Your Sidekick*, and the card says, "See the LGBTQ+ booth for more information." The signed copy is at the LGBTQ+ booth with a card that says, "See the Chinese booth for more information."

"Got it." Rowan starts moving her mech drawings to cover Katie's poster and the book information card.

"On it." Henry hits play on his phone, and the screeching sounds of Chinese opera blares from his speakers. "To be or not to be . . ."

"Why are we hiding again?" Katie asks, not bothering to keep her voice down.

Luckily, Henry's *Hamlet* speech with Chinese opera in the background is so loud that it's not like anyone can hear her.

"We're in the wrong booth." I shift a little, but it doesn't help the cramp in my calves.

"I know that." Katie sounds exasperated. "I mean, why would it be so bad if Ms. Tucker found out we're helping out with the Chinese booth?"

"Do you want to explain why you're here after getting a hundred signatures to start the LGBTQ+ booth?"

"Point taken," she grumbles. "I just can't believe we have to do this until Rainbow Fair."

"Just one more week." By then, I'm going to have killer leg muscles.

Rowan's frantic face peers down at us. "Ms. Tucker is coming our way! What should I do?"

"Just act normal," I whisper.

"To sleep, perchance to dream—ay, there's the rub," Henry

belts out just as cymbals ring out through the speakers.

"You too, Henry," Katie adds.

Well, as normal as a Song dynasty warrior reciting *Hamlet* to Chinese opera in a gym can be.

"What is this?" Ms. Tucker almost has to yell to make herself heard.

My palms grow sweaty, and my calves are burning.

Henry just keeps going with his speech, so it's Rowan who answers Ms. Tucker. "Henry is doing a *Hamlet* retelling set in the Song dynasty."

"Isn't it a bit loud, dear?"

To her credit, Rowan doesn't even glance down at us. "I think it's supposed to be that way. Culturally, I mean. And, um, historically."

"Oh, I see." She still sounds uncertain. "And what are these . . . robot drawings?" Ms. Tucker's voice firms. "As I told the other members of the robotics club, the purpose of Rainbow Fair is to celebrate the beauty of diverse cultures, and that does not mean robots."

"Actually," Rowan says, "these drawings are based on Chinese mythology." *Good for Rowan.* "This story, for example, is super interesting." Excitement vibrates through her voice.

Shoot. Rowan can go on forever once she gets started on

Chinese myths. No way can my calves last through her retelling an epic myth.

"These magpie mechs tell the story of—" Rowan stops when Katie unsubtly nudges her leg. Katie's calves must be killing her too. "Um," Rowan says, "maybe I should keep the story a surprise for Rainbow Fair."

More cymbals clash from the speakers, and Henry slams his helmet/skull onto the table for extra emphasis.

"Well, have fun," Ms. Tucker says weakly.

I hold my breath, trying to listen for Ms. Tucker's footsteps under the high-pitched sounds of the opera singers.

"Is Ms. Tucker gone yet?" Katie asks.

Rowan peers down at us. "All clear!"

Henry finishes up his speech, panting a little, and turns off the Chinese opera.

Katie and I stand, and I stretch out my tight muscles while looking around to make sure Ms. Tucker is out of sight.

"You know, Sophie," Katie comments, "when you said we had to keep this quiet, I didn't think you meant literally hiding from teachers."

I wince. "Sorry."

"No, no. It's subversive. I like it." She lifts Rowan's Asian mech drawings off the gender unicorn poster she's translating into Mandarin with the help of her parents. "I like these drawings too, Rowan."

"Thanks!" She points at one that looks like a robot dragon. "I think I'm going to make a comic out of them after Rainbow Fair is over."

Henry turns on the Chinese opera music and starts rehearsing his lines again.

Other kids passing by our booth stop to stare. Pretty soon, they're gathering around and asking questions.

"Why are you dressed like that, and is that a real sword?" one kid asks.

Henry shakes his head and continues with his speech.

"These are awesome drawings." That's a kid from Rowan's robotics club. "Why haven't you shown us these before?"

"Thanks!" Rowan beams. "I just started doing them. They're robots inspired by Chinese mythology." She points to the drawing the kid is holding. "That one is the rabbit who lives on the moon."

"What is that noise?" another kid asks. "It sounds like dying cats."

Henry turns off the music. "It's Chinese opera," he explains. "The sounds are supposed to clash. It's dramatic and tense. That's why I chose it for my version of *Hamlet*."

"Oh, that's so cool. Maybe we can do your play for drama next year."

I look around at the growing crowd of kids, and warmth fills me. Rowan and Henry are finally getting the recognition they deserve.

Katie nudges me. "You know that you did this, right?"

"Me?" I stare at her in surprise. "Rowan's the one who did the mech drawings, and Henry is the one who wrote a whole freaking *Hamlet* adaptation." I have a sneaking suspicion that he's planning on reciting the entire play at Rainbow Fair. It's only a week away, but if anyone can have all the lines memorized by then, it's Henry.

"You're the one who encouraged us to do the Chinese booth our own way." Katie gestures to the walls where Rowan's Chinese mythology robot drawings are hanging next to Katie's poster of Chinese LGBTQ+ activists and authors. "So, yeah, this is all your doing."

She's looking at me like I really did something special, and a fuzzy warmth forms in my body. I'm used to *Katie* being the one in our friendship who makes things happen. Not me. "You're the one who created the LGBTQ+ booth. And Anna is the one who had the idea of a Muslim booth showing how diverse we are. I just wanted a booth that showed everyone there's more than one way to be Chinese. And you, Rowan, and

Henry have put as much as I have into the Chinese booth. All I'm doing is using my Muslim booth stuff for this booth too."

"That's what I'm doing too—using my LGBTQ+ stuff for the Chinese booth because that's who I am." A small smile forms on Katie's lips. "Like I said, you inspired us, Sophie, and you should be proud of all this."

I look around the booth of mech drawings and Shakespeare props. Maybe Katie is right that this is something to be proud of. And maybe my parents will think so too.

For the first time since we were assigned our Rainbow Fair booths, it feels as if a weight has been lifted from my heart.

"Hi, everyone."

I turn to see Allie standing there, and my happy glow fades. "Hi, Allie." She probably wants Katie back at the LGBTQ+ booth. Like me, Katie is splitting her time between two booths.

"Is it time already?" Katie asks.

"No." She scuffs her shoe on the ground. "The thing is that Ms. Tucker was just at our booth and asking where you were. We said you went to the bathroom."

Oops. If Ms. Tucker goes to the Muslim booth and finds me gone too, she might put two and two together. Katie and I look at each other with wide eyes. "I have to get to the Muslim booth," I say, panic rising in me.

"And I should get to the LGBTQ+ booth." Katie is already moving around the booth. "Coming, Allie?"

She shakes her head. "If Ms. Tucker sees us together, it will be obvious that I came and got you." Allie is being surprisingly supportive of Katie splitting her time with the LGBTQ+ booth.

But I don't have time to wonder about what Allie might be up to. I wave goodbye to Katie, Rowan, and Henry. "Got to go. See you tomorrow."

I'm about to bolt toward the Muslim booth, but then Allie says to me, "I actually told Ms. Tucker that I was going over to the Muslim booth to see you."

"Me?" Surprise floods me.

"I said I owed you an apology," she mumbles.

Ah. I know it was just an excuse and that she wasn't really planning to apologize, but some of the frozenness I've been feeling around her starts to thaw. I start walking, and she falls into step beside me. "That was good thinking, Allie."

She looks away. "It's too bad I didn't get to see what you were doing for the Chinese booth."

Allie is clearly trying to be nice, but I'm sure she was expecting something like Rowan's mech drawings or Henry's Shakespeare retelling. "I haven't put my stuff up yet anyway. It's actually back at my other booth. I'm reusing my Muslim booth display for the Chinese booth too." I was going to do two different displays, but in the end, I found there wasn't really a difference. Like Katie, I couldn't divide who I am in half. I'm Chinese Muslim, and those identities can't be separated.

"Oh," Allie says, and there's a moment of awkward silence. "Can I come and see what you're doing at the Muslim booth, then?"

"Um, sure." I shift my backpack and feel my skin turn damp with sweat. *Calm down, Sophie.* Megan probably pressured Allie into looking at my display. Allie and I are going to make awkward conversation on the way to the Muslim booth, and then she's going to spend another thirty seconds looking at my maps and posters, and then we'll make even more awkward conversation. It's not like she's going to go all mean-girl on me. Probably not, anyway.

"How have you been?" she asks.

"Fine." Is the walk from the Chinese booth to the Muslim booth always this long? "How have you been?"

"Good."

Darn. It's my turn now. Should I ask about her booth? No, I was just there with Katie yesterday. Plus, maybe the booth is a sore subject. I'm not really sure how Allie feels about me talking Katie into secretly working on the Chinese booth.

Allie stops and turns to me. "Sophie, I wanted to say I'm sorry for what I said at the last club meeting."

I blink at her. "You already apologized."

She flushes. "Yeah, but I really mean it now."

Does that mean that she didn't mean it before? *Yeah, probably.* But it doesn't matter. I've done some things I've regretted too. The tension in my neck unknots. "It's okay." I start walking again, and Allie matches my pace. "I guess we should try to get along since we're both friends with Katie."

Her face turns even more red. "Actually, I was hoping you and I could be friends too."

My mouth drops. I *definitely* was not expecting that, but I don't have to think about it too hard. "Yeah, that would be good."

She smiles, the relief obvious on her face. "Are you coming to the mall with Katie, Megan, Shane, and me next weekend?"

Katie already invited me, but I turned her down because of the weirdness with Allie. "Thanks, but I made plans with Anna." Next weekend is right after Rainbow Fair, so Anna and I won't have the booth to work on anymore, but it would still be fun to hang out with her.

We approach the Muslim booth, and Anna waves at us. "Hi, Sophie and Allie!"

Allie waves back. "Why don't you both come, and we can all hang out?"

All of us? My best friend, my new friend, and Katie's new friends? A smile spreads over my face. "I'll ask Anna, but I think that would be fine." In fact, it could be better than fine.

It could be perfect.

Twenty-One

I take a deep breath as I push open the front door of my house. Enough with this silly deception about being in two booths. It's time to come clean to my parents. But when I step inside the house, the smell of bleach and disinfectant hits me in the face.

"Sophie!" Mom greets me with a spray bottle in one hand and a bucket dangling from her arm. "I'm so glad you're home."

"What's going on?" I take off my shoes and start to put them in the shoe tray, except it's missing and the hardwood floor of the entryway is gleaming.

Dad runs by wearing rubber gloves and holding a sponge. "Put your shoes in the closet please. We're cleaning."

"Yeah, I got that." I put my shoes and jacket in the closet. There's a sour taste in my mouth, and it's not because of the cleaning products in the air. It's because I remember the last time my parents cleaned this hard. "Let me guess. Shūshu, Āyí, and Cousin Nina are coming over." My dad's younger brother, his wife, and my snooty cousin Nina live in California, but every year they come up for a visit with pretty much zero notice. "When are they coming?"

Mom eyes the random piles of clutter in the living room with a look of defeat. "In one hour."

"One hour?" I squeak. "When did you find out they were coming, and why didn't you tell me?" I would have expected them to text me with a frantic message to come home and help clean right away.

"We didn't want to interrupt your Chinese booth preparations."

"Oh." Guilt twinges in me. There's this weird competition thing between my parents and Nina's where they passive-aggressively brag about their offspring. Like me, Nina gets straight As in school, but unlike me, she also speaks perfect Chinese and even attended a Chinese language and culture immersion program in Taiwan last summer. All I have going for me is the Chinese booth. It would be fair to say that my parents are on a losing streak. "Do you want me to mop something?" I ask.

"No time." Mom shoves the spray bottle and bucket into my hands. "I have to finish making dinner. Just clear the mess in the living room and put stuff into the closets. Dust what you can if you have time."

"On it." I start by putting the spray bottle and bucket into the entryway closet. It's looking pretty full, so I'll have to spread the junk in the living room between the hallway closet, my parents' bedroom closet, and my own bedroom closet. I'm going to have to clean up my own bedroom too.

My heart sinks at the thought of Nina, who looks like she stepped out of a fashion magazine, making snide comments about my Wonder Woman–themed bedroom. Nina is only two years older than me, but she always treats me like a kid. If she's not making snobby comments on my room or clothes, Nina pretty much ignores me on her visits. The one and only time Nina met Katie, she ignored her too.

After listening to Nina laugh and talk in Chinese to the adults, Katie whispered to me, "We hate her, right?"

Regretfully, I said, "I'm technically not allowed to hate my own cousin."

"No problem," Katie replied. "I'll hate her enough for both of us."

I wish Katie were here now.

A few sprints later and haphazard stuffing of closets mean that the mess in the living room has magically disappeared. There's not really much time to dust, but Mom said to do that only if there's time.

I look around the living room in satisfaction. It looks pretty good if I do say so myself. Then I spot the blue spines of the Quran on the top shelf of the bookcase and remember how dusty the English version was. I go to the full closet and manage to extract a clean dustcloth without toppling the piles of junk I had just thrown in there.

I take the Quran in English from the bookshelf and gently wipe off the cover with the soft cloth.

"What are you doing, Sophie?"

I turn to see my father peering at me. He's taken off the rubber gloves and changed out of his old jeans and T-shirt and into a nice sweater and pants, so our hour must almost be up.

I put down the dustcloth and try to sound casual. "I just noticed that this Quran was dusty."

He shakes his head. "We shouldn't have let it get dusty. Were you looking at it?"

"Um, no. I mean, I didn't read it or anything."

He smiles. "You can if you want."

I hesitate. "I wasn't sure if I should."

Dad walks over to me and touches the cover of the Quran in my hands. "Your mother and I don't read this one," he says. "It's easier for us to read in Chinese."

"Okay," I say, not sure where he's going with this.

"Of course you can read it," Dad says gently. "Why do you

think we have a Quran in English?"

I stare at him in wonder. "Is it for me?"

"Yes, Sophie. This Quran is for you."

My mother's voice calls out from the kitchen, asking if he knows where they put the fancy-company chopsticks.

"Read the Quran whenever you want, Sophie," he tells me. "It will be here for you."

He leaves, and I stand still, looking at the gilded book in my hands.

Slowly, I open the blue cover and turn the thin paper to the first page.

Nina perches on the edge of my Wonder Woman bedspread like she's afraid the Amazon princess is going to come to life and lasso her, but maybe that's just my own fantasy.

"So, what have you been up to?" The question would seem almost nice if I ignored the fact that Nina isn't even looking at me but examining her beautifully manicured blood-red nails instead.

"Well, there's this Rainbow Fair at school—"

She laughs. "I thought you were in middle school. That sounds like some little-kid thing."

Anger boils up in me. I don't care if I've made fun of Rainbow Fair for two years in a row. It's different when Nina does it. "It's actually really cool," I say stiffly. "In fact, this year's Rainbow Fair is going to be legendary."

"If you say so," she says in a bored voice.

"Girls," my mom calls out from the dining room. "It's time for dinner."

"Coming!" I call back in relief.

Nina rises gracefully to her feet. "Láile!" Of course she had to show me up by saying the same thing I did but in Chinese.

When we reach the dining room, the smells of garlic and ginger float toward us. Mom ended up ordering takeout for most of the dinner, but she made her own dumplings since most restaurant dumplings are pork. Hers are filled with ground beef and a special garlic, ginger, and chives mix.

Nina compliments Mom (in Chinese, of course), and then everyone but me is speaking in Chinese as we sit down around the table. I understand a little over half of what they're saying, but at least my uncle and aunt's questions to me are always the same and easy to answer.

"Xuéxiào hǎo ma?" How is school?

"Hǎo." Fine.

My parents' questions to Nina are more complex. They're more like, "How is that . . . wonderful something, something, something . . . going?"

And Nina's replies are like, "Oh, Aunt and Uncle, thank you

for asking about the . . . something, something, something. . . . Couldn't be better!"

My aunt and uncle have finished their basic questions for me and are now basking in the reflected glory of whatever my cousin is talking about. Just once, I wish my parents didn't have to just listen and smile politely while Nina shows off.

I wish I could do something they would be proud of.

"Nina works too hard," my uncle says in Chinese, breaking into my cousin's flow of accomplishments. "She should be more like Sophie."

I gape at him, stomach knotting. Did my own uncle just low-key burn me?

Mom stiffens, and Dad glances at me with worry in his eyes, so yeah—my uncle definitely *did* imply I was an underachieving loser.

Nina smiles smugly, speaking in English the way she always does when she's about to throw me under the bus. "Sophie has been telling me about her school's Rainbow Fair."

Anger floods me. She only brought up Rainbow Fair because she thinks it's childish and wants to show me up.

"Sophie has been working very hard on the Chinese booth," Mom says with a pointed look at my uncle.

"Oh, what will she be doing for the booth?" my aunt asks politely.

"She says it's a secret and won't even tell us, but it's sure to be fantastic," Dad says proudly.

Heat rises into my face. "It's nothing much," I mumble.

"Really?" Nina asks in a fake innocent voice. "Because I thought you said it was going to be *legendary*."

Katie was totally right. I don't care if Nina is my cousin—we *do* hate her.

Dad's face lights up. "I knew it, Sophie! You're going to do calligraphy of the poetry of the eight immortals."

"Or maybe a dragon," Mom says excitedly. "Didn't you make that wonderful papier-mâché dragon last year?"

Yeah, except that was all Katie. This year, she teamed up with Shane to make a bunch of papier-mâché unicorns for the LGBTQ+ booth, though there will be a unicorn for the Chinese booth too. Along with a *Hamlet* soliloquy to a dead guy's helmet, a robo comic, not to mention my own family history of being Hui on display. I *think* my parents will like that last part, at least, but it's a stretch to call any of it legendary.

"How wonderful," my aunt says, but I can tell she doesn't really think the Chinese booth will measure up to anything Nina has done. "You'll have to take lots of pictures and send them to us."

"Oh, we definitely will." The steel in Mom's voice tells me that I am about to experience picture-taking on a whole new level. My heart drops. I have a feeling that pictures of gender unicorn posters in Mandarin or robo comics inspired by Chinese martial arts fantasies won't score my parents any points.

My uncle nudges Nina. "That is the kind of creative approach to school that will make you successful." Maybe my uncle isn't so bad after all.

For once, Nina looks like she's at a loss for words.

My parents are beaming at me and waiting for my answer.

I fiddle with my chopsticks as sweat beads on my forehead. How am I supposed to tell my parents about the subversive Chinese booth *now*? They're expecting the poetry of the eight immortals in calligraphy and a papier-mâché dragon—in other words, a *traditional* Chinese booth that will make them look good in the eyes of their relatives. But I don't think my actual Chinese booth will gain them any bragging rights. I can't explain this to Mom and Dad in front of Nina and her parents. Maybe it will be better to just wait and show them my booths at Rainbow Fair.

"Um, it's going to be a surprise."

"I can't wait," my parents say together in perfect unison.

Great. Just great.

Twenty-Two

I thought the picture-taking on Parent-Teacher Night was overkill, but it's nothing compared to the day of Rainbow Fair.

"Don't you both look lovely!" Mom is beaming at Katie and me as Dad takes another picture of us at the entrance of the school.

This time, we're not the only family hovering in the entrance of the school. All around us are parents, including the Yangs, taking pictures.

Katie is wearing the purple qípáo with embroidered peonies that I picked out for her, and I'm wearing a midnight-blue qípáo with embroidered silver phoenixes.

I hate to brag, but Mom is right. We look amazing. Katie and I grin at each other and then lean into each other to pose for another picture.

"I suppose you should get to your booth," Dad says, putting his phone away.

"We can't wait to see it." Mom is practically bouncing on her toes.

My smile slips. Will my parents still be proud of me when they see what I've done?

"We're excited to see your booths," Ms. Yang adds.

Katie glances at me and slips her arm through mine. "Yeah, speaking of that, Sophie and I need to finish setting up our booth."

"You mean *booths*. Plural." Mr. Yang's smile looks forced. "Since the two of you aren't in the same booth this year."

I stiffen, not knowing what to say. This would be the perfect time to tell our parents that we're both doing the Chinese booth. But then that might get into messy questions about breaking the rule against doing more than one booth. Katie's parents won't care; they'll just be delighted that she's doing the Chinese booth. But mine have always been more of the "follow the rules and don't make trouble" kind of parents. I know I have to tell them, but I kind of want them to see the Chinese and Muslim booths first. The truth is that I *am* proud of both booths. And I want my parents to see that for themselves. Maybe they'll understand then why I broke the rules.

Katie flashes me an understanding look. "Right, right." She's pulling me along with her as she scoots us away from our parents. She knows I want my parents to see the booths before

I explain what I've done, and I think she might want to surprise her parents too. "Booths. Totally different ones. Sophie is in the Chinese booth, and I am in the LGBTQ+ booth."

"That is correct." I try to smile, but I think it comes out more as a panicked baring of teeth. "We really need to set up our two separate booths now."

"Okay, we'll be back in an hour!" Mom calls out as Katie and I rush through the main entrance of the school.

I turn to Katie as soon as the doors swing shut behind us. "What was that?" I demand. "I really thought you'd be better at this."

"Me? What about you?" She mimics me saying "That is correct" in a robotic voice.

Laughter bubbles up in me. "Can we agree that neither of us is secret-agent material?"

"Ooh, who's a secret agent?"

I turn to see Anna with her usual smile. "Not us, apparently." I hook my arm through hers so the three of us are linked together. "Let's go do Rainbow Fair!"

As soon as the three of us step foot in the gym, I can tell that something is different. For one thing, Ms. Tucker is running around with a megaphone, shouting frantically, "Everyone get back in their booths, please!" She ducks around a huge papier-mâché puppet of what looks like a cross between a purple snake and a cartoon dinosaur. "The parents will be here in an hour!"

I stop cold, and Katie and Anna stop with me. "What's going on?"

Kids are running from booth to booth, talking excitedly.

Shane comes running . . . galloping up in a fuzzy white unicorn costume with pink ribbons streaming from their hair. "Katie, Sophie, Anna—this is the best Rainbow Fair ever!"

"Did the dunk tank get approved?" Katie asks blankly.

They shake their pink mane. "Even better. Everyone's doing cool things. Kids are doing awesome performances and art."

"All the booths?" Anna asks.

"Not the booths, exactly," Shane replies. "We're kind of outside the booths now. Thanks to you!" I think Shane is talking about Katie, but they're looking at me.

"What do you mean?" I ask.

"Well, we all saw the way you refused to be boxed into just one booth, Sophie. And you did too, Katie." Shane is beaming at both of us now. "The connections you made between the booths are so great, and everyone was inspired by what you've done. Megan went off with the Norwegian kids to do some kind of queer Valhalla skit—don't ask me to explain. You'll have to see it. And the last I saw Allie, she was going around and handing out resource pamphlets and rainbow stickers."

Katie grins and nudges me. "I told you that you changed Rainbow Fair."

I open my mouth to protest, but the papier-mâché puppet careens out of the way of a few kids, and I have to admit that this *is* different. I point at the purple snake/dinosaur. "I have to ask. What is that?"

Shane squints at the puppet. "Well, it came from the Scottish booth, so I'm guessing it's the Loch Ness Monster? I've always thought the Loch Ness Monster was cool, but that looks more like Barney than Nessie. I did the Scottish booth last year, so maybe I should go help them." Shane starts walking over to the group of kids struggling to carry their purple puppet but then pauses to call out over their shoulder. "Oh, and by the way, watch where you step."

My eyes widen. "Why should—"

Rowan comes racing over with a remote control in her hand. Something bumps into my shoe, and I look down to see a rabbit robot, just a few inches tall. There's an outline of a full moon behind the rabbit and a tiny little mortar and pestle attached to the paws of the rabbit. Obviously, this is Rowan's take on the Chinese story of the rabbit on the moon pounding the ingredients for the potion of long life. "Oops," she says happily. "Tùzǐ got away from me."

"What is that?" Anna asks.

"'Tùzǐ' means 'rabbit' in Chinese," I explain.

"I think Anna is asking why there's a rabbit robot being chased by another rabbit robot," Katie says dryly.

She's right. That's the bigger question.

Another rabbit robot zooms by with Carter, one of Rowan's robotics club friends, running after it and flipping switches on his remote.

"Carter doesn't have as much control over his rabbit," Rowan says.

"I thought Ms. Tucker didn't approve the robots for Rainbow Fair." I watch as the runaway rabbit crashes into the wall behind the Norwegian booth, which is empty. "I mean, I get Tùzǐ since there's the rabbit in the moon Chinese myth, but what's with the other rabbits?"

"It turns out there are Celtic myths about rabbits too," Rowan says. Another rabbit robot zips by. "Actually, it's surprising how many cultures have rabbit myths. It would be fun to get them together and tell all the rabbit stories . . . if we can find them all."

"Almiraj!" Anna claps. "That's a rabbit story my parents used to tell me."

Rowan's eyes light up. "I've got extra robots. Come on—let's go make your rabbit."

Anna glances at me, clearly torn. "Aren't we supposed to stay at the Muslim booth?"

"Go on," I say, slipping my arm from hers. "No one else is in their booths."

Anna grins at me and steps over Tùzĭ toward Rowan. "Almiraj is a yellow hare with a black horn," she says to Rowan. "Can you do that?"

"Not a problem." She flicks a switch, and Tùzĭ takes off again with Anna and Rowan right behind it.

Katie and I look at each other. "Let's go look around," we say at the same time.

The first booth we find that actually has kids there is the Black culture booth. Lucas and a few other kids from the Black Student Union are behind a table full of books, neatly displayed with information cards. Behind them is a revolving book rack that looks like it was borrowed from the library, and it's filled with even more books by Black authors.

The booth is amazing, and I'm not the only one who thinks so. There are about a dozen kids who are looking at books and asking questions.

"Hi, Sophie, hi, Katie," Lucas says when he spots us.

"Your booth looks incredible!" Katie says.

"It really is cool." I beam at Lucas. "Much better than what Ms. Tucker wanted you to do."

"Thanks," Lucas says, "and look—the books the two of you told me about are right here in front, and kids have been asking us about them. A bunch of them said they were going to check out the Muslim and the LGBTQ+ booths." He waves a hand at *All You Have to Do* and *You Should See Me in a Crown*, both displayed prominently on book stands with an information card.

A swell of emotion crests over me. "I love this so much."

"Me too." Katie puts a hand on her heart. "Maybe kids who wouldn't have gone to our booths before will go take a look now."

She's right, especially about the Muslim booth. Like Allie, most kids probably think of Muslims as all super conservative and oppressed by our religion. But now, because of the book displays at the Black culture and the LGBTQ+ booths, they might get a different idea of Muslims, and maybe they'll visit our booth to learn more.

Another robo rabbit zips by, and Lucas looks after it enviously. "Where are those coming from?"

"The Chinese booth," Katie replies.

"Rowan, a sixth grader, is the one making them," I add.

"She's at the Chinese booth now, making one for Anna, but I'm sure she'll make one for you."

"Thanks!" Lucas tells his boothmates he'll be back and then hurries off, probably worried that Rowan will give all the rabbits away before he can get one.

"I'll bet you anything that Henry is going to write a rabbit play after Rainbow Fair is over," Katie comments.

"I'm not going to take that bet."

My attention is caught by Lucas almost running into Ms. Tucker, who's coming down an aisle with wisps of hair escaping its neat bob. "Be careful!"

"Sorry, Ms. Tucker!" he calls back without slowing down.

Her mouth opens like she's about to tell him to stop, but then her gaze lands on us, and she strides over. My stomach sinks when I see that she's clutching a robo-rabbit in one hand.

"Where is Rowan?" she asks grimly.

"Um . . . ," I say, panicked.

"Bathroom?" Katie says like she's trying out an answer out loud. "Yeah, that's right. I think Rowan went to the bathroom." She's almost as bad as me at lying to adults.

A kid runs up with a relieved smile. "Oh good! You found our trickster rabbit!"

"Jesse, aren't you supposed to be in the Indigenous booth?" Ms. Tucker asks.

"I am, but our rabbit escaped."

I think Ms. Tucker is going to protest, but she just sighs and hands over the rabbit. "Keep a better eye on it and get back to your booth, please. The parents will be here soon."

"Thanks!" Jesse runs off, and I'm pretty sure there's no chance they're going back to their booth.

Ms. Tucker smooths down her hair and looks at us. "Why aren't you two at the Chinese booth?"

"I'm in the LGBTQ+ booth," Katie reminds her.

"And I'm in the Muslim booth," I say.

"Oh right." She looks flustered. "Why aren't you in those booths, then?"

"There's no one else there," Katie explains. "The others are helping with other projects."

"And Anna is with Rowan, getting an Almiraj." I have only a vague idea of what that is, but I'm pretty sure Ms. Tucker won't know either.

"I give up! It's all chaos anyway." Ms. Tucker throws up her hands. "All I wanted was for you kids to get in touch with your culture."

Irritation sparks in me. "That is what we're doing," I say. "It just looks a little different." The Loch Ness Monster puppet comes by at that moment with Shane as one of the kids holding it up, and I don't know how they did it so quickly, but the puppet looks way less Barney and more Nessie. And also twice the original size. "Okay, maybe it's a lot different, but that could be a good thing."

Katie gives Ms. Tucker an unsympathetic look. "At least kids are having fun at Rainbow Fair for once."

Ms. Tucker gapes at her. I take Katie's arm and start to drag her away before she says something that gets her in trouble. "We should go find Rowan."

"Could you at least tell Rowan to stop handing out rabbit robots?" Ms. Tucker asks.

"Sure," I say.

"No problem," Katie says.

We turn and walk away. "Are you going to tell Rowan to stop making rabbit robots?" I ask Katie.

"Not a chance," she says.

"Me neither."

We grin at each other and loop our arms together. "Let's go see what else is new about Rainbow Fair," Katie says.

As the Loch Ness Monster, rainbow unicorn puppets, and mythological robo-rabbits race by, I start to think that this might be a very different Rainbow Fair.

And as I told Ms. Tucker—that is a good thing, indeed.

Twenty-Three

I'm having such a good time exploring the new and improved and definitely more chaotic Rainbow Fair that I almost forget to be anxious about my parents. Almost. "What time is it?" I ask Katie.

She checks her phone. "We still have fifteen minutes before the parents come, but I should go find Shane, Megan, and Allie anyway."

"Right," I say. "I'm going to go to meet my parents at the entrance and take them to the Chinese booth, where my display of Hui culture is. I think that will ease them into finding out that I've been breaking the rules by unofficially doing the Chinese booth while I've been officially co-running the Muslim booth."

This must be the ninety-ninth time Katie has heard me repeat my plan. She looks around at all the kids walking down the aisles and talking excitedly about Rowan's rabbits or Megan's queer Valhalla skit. "Do you really think your parents are going to care that you were doing two booths when everyone has clearly broken out of all our booths?"

"Maybe not." I think about the pride in their eyes as they bragged about me to my uncle and aunt and speculated about my "legendary" Chinese booth. "But I still want to show them the Chinese booth and explain why I did it this way."

Katie nods. "You've got this, Sophie."

My stomach knots with nervous excitement. "I hope so."

Waving goodbye to Katie, I start walking quickly to the gym's entrance. Knowing my parents, it's likely that they will be—

I stop cold. *Early.* My parents are standing right in front of the Muslim booth.

Of course my parents would be early. Anxiety washes over me even though I'm not even sure what I'm worried about. *They are proud about being Muslim.* But that doesn't mean they want their personal faith splashed all over a wall in a booth for everyone to see.

"Mom, Dad—what are you doing here?"

My laptop is on the table, playing a scene from *Ms. Marvel* where Kamala is getting advice from her imam, but my parents aren't looking at the video. All their attention is on my display of Hui culture on the wall.

Dad traces a line on the colorful map. It's the one that leads from the former Ottoman Empire to China. "So this is why you asked where our family is from." His voice sounds all choked up.

Mom traces a line from China to Taiwan on the map. "And this is why you asked me why your great-grandparents left China." She reads the information about oppression of Chinese Muslims in silence and turns to me. "But I never told you that. How did you know that was the reason my grandparents moved with me from China to Taiwan?"

At least she's not asking me why our family journey is in the Muslim booth instead of the Chinese booth. "It was just what I researched." My voice is shaky. "Is that why our family left China?"

"Yes," she whispers. "That's a part of it."

Dad puts an arm around Mom. "I think it's true for my grandparents too."

I stare at the two of them. "So, um, you're not mad that I did this?"

Mom looks puzzled. "Why would we be mad?"

"It's a good thing to know your family's history and to share it," Dad says. "Of course we're not angry."

Mom frowns. "I still don't understand why you didn't tell us about all this."

"Well." I inhale a breath. "You might not have noticed, but

this is the Muslim booth, and there's that rule against doing more than one booth. I did put the Hui cultural display in the Chinese booth there too." My chest squeezes tight. "The point is that I'm in the Muslim booth." *And not the Chinese booth.* I don't say that part out loud, but I'm sure my parents have figured it out.

"That makes sense to me," Mom says.

Dad nods. "You are Muslim, after all."

"But then if you're okay with all this," I blurt out, "then why don't you ever talk about being Muslim around other people?"

Mom flushes, and Dad looks away uncomfortably.

I want to tell them how confusing this all is and explain that I did the booth to figure out what it means for me to be Muslim, but the words are stuck in my throat.

The next slide on my laptop comes up, and it's an image of Anna and me under the white awnings behind the mosque, with the family we met there. When we told them about our Rainbow Fair booth, they insisted that we take a picture together to use in our slideshow. Their warmth and Anna's brightness practically radiates from the picture, which isn't surprising. What surprises me is how happy I look in the picture. Like I belong.

My parents are looking at me instead of my slideshow, and I want to point out the picture, but the slideshow moves on to a screenshot from the *Ms. Marvel* comics. It's a page from the Kamala Khan–Wolverine team-up issue, which doesn't really have anything to do with Islamic culture other than Kamala being a Muslim superhero, but this storyline is just so darn cool that I couldn't resist.

I wish my parents saw the picture of me at the barbecue, but more than that—I wish I had brought them with me.

Dad opens his mouth, and I think he's going to answer my questions about why they don't talk about being Muslim in public, but at that moment, Anna dashes over with her parents in tow.

It's impossible not to be happy to see Anna, but I wonder what my dad was going to say.

"Are these your parents, Sophie?" Anna's voice quickens. "I've been wanting to meet them."

"Um, yes," I say, anxiety fluttering in my stomach. I hope Anna's parents don't reveal we've already met. "Anna, Mr. Demir and Ms. Demir—these are my parents."

"Hello, Mr. Hu and Ms. Hu." Anna gives them her usual bright smile.

The adults all exchange their first names, and then Mr. Demir says, "Sophie and this booth is all that Anna talks about. You must be so proud of your daughter."

Now I'm hoping my parents don't reveal that I haven't

mentioned Anna before. The flutter in my stomach shifts into full-on churning.

My dad puts a hand on my shoulder. "Of course."

"Yes. We are so happy to meet you and Anna too." Mom manages to both smile at the Demirs and give me a sharp look at the same time. Yeah, she's definitely going to give me a hard time later about not mentioning Anna. I can see her point since the Demirs clearly know all about me already.

Dad turns to the booth. "I don't think we've seen everything in here yet."

"Make sure you look at Anna's poster about the hijab," I say. "It's amazing."

She blushes. "It's just a poster about the reasons a girl might choose to wear a hijab," she says, "and it explains why it's a personal spiritual choice."

"Oh, I've been wanting to see that poster," Ms. Demir says.

Both sets of parents move over to the poster. Next to the poster is a prayer rug that Anna decided to display after all. Mom touches the prayer rug. "My mother had a rug like this one." Her voice is soft with memories. "I wish I still had it, but it was so worn that it just fell apart."

Ms. Demir smiles, and I can see where Anna gets her incredible smile from. "I know of a shop where you can get a new one."

"Maybe." Mom smiles back.

Pretty soon, our parents are all chatting as if they've been friends for years.

"Where is your yellow rabbit with the black horn?" I ask Anna. "I wanted to see it."

"Rowan is still working on it, so it's at the Chinese booth. We should go there after our parents are finished looking at this booth."

Our parents are now exchanging embarrassing childhood stories about us and laughing so loudly they probably can't hear what we're talking about.

"Everything okay with your parents now?" Anna asks.

I look at my parents laughing and talking with Anna's parents. "I think it is, actually."

"Good." Is it my imagination, or has Anna lost a bit of her sparkle?

I clear my throat. "Are *you* okay?"

"Well, it's just that . . ." She twists the ends of her long hair. "I know you have Katie and everything, but I thought we were becoming friends too."

I stare at her in confusion. Where is this coming from? "Of course we're friends."

She looks me right in the eye. "I know you didn't want to tell your parents that you weren't doing the Chinese booth, but

I didn't realize that you didn't mention me at all."

Oh. When she put it that way—it sounds pretty bad. "You're right." I swallow past the tightness in my throat. "I'm sorry that I didn't tell my parents I was working on the Muslim booth with you and that I didn't say you're my friend. I was so caught up in not disappointing my parents that I kept things from them that I didn't need to." I'm not even sure I understand the choices I made, but I do know one thing. My heart twists. "I'm sorry I hurt you. Just for the record, meeting you and becoming your friend has been the all-time coolest thing that has happened to me this year."

"Really?" Her face lights up. "I thought that since you and Katie are such good friends, maybe you didn't really need me."

I shake my head. "I *do* need you." I don't know how to explain how much it means to me to be able to talk to Anna about being Muslim, but it's more than that. I just love her warmth and cheerfulness. For the first time in my life, I consider the possibility of having more than one best friend. Reaching over to hug Anna, I say, "You're awesome, and I'm so lucky to have you as a friend."

She sniffles and hugs me back tight. "I'm lucky too."

Twenty-Four

When Anna and I bring my parents and hers to the Chinese booth, we find Katie there, too, with her parents.

Dad says hello to the Yangs and starts taking pictures of my Hui display, Rowan's art, Katie's poster, and Henry's *Hamlet* props. "I can't wait until your shūshu and āyí see these," he says enthusiastically.

Happiness flutters in my chest. I don't know what my uncle and aunt are going to make of these pictures, but it doesn't matter. What matters is that my parents are proud of what I've done.

"Where are Rowan and Henry?" I ask Katie.

"Henry got a tip that someone might have a skull he can use for his *Hamlet* performance, and Rowan is in high demand. *Everyone* wants a robo-rabbit. Speaking of that . . ." Katie presents a yellow rabbit with a black horn to Anna with a flourish. "Rowan told me to give this to you if you came by."

"Thank you!" Anna claps and takes the rabbit.

"What is that?" Mr. Demir asks, peering at the little robot.

"It's Almiraj!" Anna says.

"Don't you recognize the one-horned mythical rabbit from poetry and legend?" Ms. Demir teases her husband.

"Of course I do," he says, mock offended. "But this one looks a little . . . mechanical."

"Apparently, one of the Chinese booth kids is in the robotics club," Mr. Yang explains. "Mythological robots! Isn't it wonderful?"

There's only one way to respond to Mr. Yang when he's in full-on enthusiastic mode.

"Yes, certainly," Ms. Demir says.

"Let me introduce you all," Mom says.

As my parents introduce the Yangs to the Demirs, I turn to Katie. "What did your parents think of your gender unicorn poster that they helped translate into Mandarin?"

She grins and points to the wall where Rowan's drawing of a mech rabbit leaping over the moon hangs. "They were over the moon about it."

Both Anna and I groan. "I think your dad is infecting you with his jokes," I say.

Ms. Yang gestures to the back wall of the booth and says, "We were just looking at Sophie's display of Chinese Muslim culture. It's really wonderful." I can tell she's thinking of the morning after the slumber party and bacon-gate.

Mom blushes, probably thinking of bacon-gate too. "Thank you," she says. "Katie's poster is wonderful too. Did you help her with the Mandarin?"

"Yes." Ms. Yang smiles. "In fact, it got us thinking. We were thinking it would be nice if Katie tried Saturday Chinese school again."

Whoa. I did not expect that from free-spirited, artsy Ms. Yang, who always insists I call her Gloria, though Mom would never let me do that in a million years.

"Mom!" Katie protests.

"Sophie should go to Chinese school too." My mom, on the other hand, is completely predictable.

There are worse things than going to Chinese school with my best—one of my best friends, but I protest on principle anyway. "Mom!"

Ms. Yang and Mom look at each other and laugh, and I wonder if they're finally on their way to becoming friends.

"What's wrong with Chinese school?" Anna asks.

"Four hours on a Saturday morning," Katie explains in a hushed voice like she's describing a dungeon complete with chains and moldy bread.

"Homework on Friday night," I add.

"Okay, I'm convinced." Anna mock shudders but ruins the effect by smiling. "So, I'm guessing you two aren't going to ditch us for Chinese school tomorrow?"

It takes me a moment to remember that Anna, Katie, and I are going to the mall with Allie, Megan, and Shane tomorrow. I smile and put my arms around both Anna and Katie. I'm not as against Chinese school as I'm pretending to be, and I suspect Katie isn't either, but for right now, all I want to do is hang out with my friends, old and new.

"I wouldn't miss it," Katie and I say in unison.

A whirring noise makes me look down, and I see one of Rowan's robot rabbits whizz by me. Dad bends down to pick it up and stares at it bemusedly until Ms. Tucker rounds the corner, spots the rabbit, and strides toward us.

"These darn rabbits," she says grimly, and I have the feeling she edited out a stronger word to describe Rowan's robots. She takes a breath and addresses the group of parents at our booth. "I am so very sorry that Rainbow Fair has been such a disaster this year. You have my assurance that the school administration will have an assembly on Monday with the students to ensure that this does not happen next year."

"I don't see it as a disaster." Dad hands the rabbit to her. "I happen to think that this year's Rainbow Fair has been outstanding."

"Even better than last year," Mom adds. That's saying something, since last year was the one she considered the Chinese booth to have "won."

"Especially with the addition of the LGBTQ+ booth," Ms. Yang says.

Mr. Yang nods. "Absolutely."

Katie smiles at her parents. "Thanks, Mom and Dad."

"This is our first Rainbow Fair," Ms. Demir says, "but it's been really great."

"I can't imagine a better Rainbow Fair," Mr. Demir agrees.

Mom has a steely look in her eyes. "It's wonderful to see the kids explore multiple aspects of their identities."

"I couldn't agree more," Dad says at once.

"It all started with Sophie," Katie chimes in.

My parents smile at me with pride, and a warm sensation wells up in me.

Anna holds up her yellow-and-black rabbit. "Rainbow Fair is definitely more fun than anything my old school had."

Ms. Tucker blinks at us as if we've all sprouted rabbit heads. "Well," she says, looking down at the robot in her hand. "I suppose it's not all bad."

On cue, Henry careens down the aisle in full Song dynasty

armor and roller skates, with speakers blaring Chinese opera taped to his chest. "To be or not to be—that is the question," he bellows.

Ms. Tucker closes her eyes and sighs.

I should just let it go—but I can't. Rowan and Henry worked hard to make the Chinese booth their own, and so did Katie and I. "Ms. Tucker," I say, "it seems like you don't like our booth."

"That's not true, Sophie," she says, sounding hurt. "I supported your Muslim booth completely." She glances at Katie, who's come to stand next to me. "And I supported Katie's LGBTQ+ booth too. In fact, shouldn't you two be getting back to your booths?"

Katie and I don't budge. "But I'm Chinese," I say, "so this is also my booth."

"Mine too." Katie puts her arm around me.

The warmth of her closeness fills me with courage. "Rainbow Fair's one-booth rule isn't working, and I think the committee needs to change it."

"Yeah, Sophie is right." Katie is looking at me with awed surprise, like she's not totally sure what's happened to her oldest friend but likes this new me too. "We'll start a petition if we need to."

Ms. Tucker's eyes dart to our parents as if she is hoping

they'll scold us for being rude to a teacher, but they're beaming. I'd expect Katie's parents to support her, but pride is shining on my parents' faces too. A lump forms in my throat.

The Demirs look puzzled, but Anna says, "I agree. Everyone should get to do whatever booths they identify with." Her parents both nod; clearly, they trust her judgment.

Anna stands on the other side of me, and I slip an arm around her waist so I'm holding my two closest friends. "And we should be able to do them however we want." I remember the way Ms. Tucker had dismissed Lucas's idea of displaying books by Black authors. "Have you been to the Black culture booth yet? It's awesome."

"Well . . . ," she says, her voice trailing off. "I haven't had a chance to see all the booths yet."

Right. That's because she's been too busy trying to herd us all back into our assigned booths.

"Maybe you should check it out now, Ms. Tucker." Katie's smile is edged.

Ms. Tucker looks at the three of us, united in our determination to make Rainbow Fair into something that's *ours*. "There's no need for a petition," she says at last. "The committee will change the rule and allow you to be in more than one booth." Her gaze lands on me, the hard lines of her face easing. "And you're right, Sophie. You should get to make the booths into whatever you want."

To my surprise, she seems to mean it. Awe hits me all at once.

I think we've managed to change Rainbow Fair.

Rainbow Fair is starting to wind down, and my parents are standing in front of my Hui culture display again, but this time it's in the Chinese booth next to Rowan's mythological mech drawings, Henry's Song dynasty set pieces for his *Hamlet* soliloquy, and Katie's gender unicorn poster translated into Mandarin.

It's funny, but my display looks like it belongs here just as much as it does next to the prayer rug and Anna's poster on the hijab.

"This is such an important part of Chinese culture," Mom tells me. "I'm so glad you're telling our family story."

The obvious question burns on my tongue. *If it's so important, then why don't my parents talk about being Hui?* They're both smiling at me, and I don't want to spoil the moment, but I need to know. "You never answered my question," I say.

Dad looks at me in confusion. "What question?"

"You're always telling me that I should be proud to be Chinese and to be Muslim." I scuff the floor with my shoe. "So why don't you ever talk about being Muslim in public?"

Dad nods gravely. "That isn't an easy question to answer," he says, "but I suppose it has something to do with how Muslims are seen here in the United States. People here didn't really know about Chinese Muslims, and it just seemed easier to let them assume that we weren't Muslim."

I remember what Anna said about a kid at her old school calling her a terrorist. I guess I can see why my parents found it safer to pass as non-Muslim.

"But we never meant to give you the impression that we are ashamed of being Muslim," he continues.

I shake my head. "I never thought that." I hesitate because everything is going so well with my parents, but maybe it's time we talked honestly and openly. "But it was confusing for me. You kept telling me I should be proud to be Muslim, but I got the feeling you wanted me to keep it quiet. Not a secret, exactly, but just something we didn't talk about."

"I can see why you would think that," Mom says regretfully. "And the truth is that it wasn't only here where people treat us differently because we're Muslim." A hard look comes into her eyes. "When I was little in Taiwan, kids would put pork in my lunch so I couldn't eat it."

"What?" Outrage thickens my voice. "That's awful!"

She shrugs, but there's still pain in her eyes. "It's just how kids are, but part of me was glad you didn't talk about being

Muslim at school. I thought it might keep you safe from being bullied like I was or worse."

Worse? But I think I already know. I'm remembering the research I had done into the re-education camps in China where Muslims are forced to give up their religion. And here in the US with Muslim travel bans and Muslims being rounded up and imprisoned and/or deported after 9/11 even though they didn't do anything wrong.

Mom looks around at the colorful booths and kids folding up tablecloths, taking down colorful posters, and packing up things from their homes. "You've really created something special here, Sophie."

Dad is looking around, too, at what I always used to think was a cheesy cultural fair in a stinky gym. But Rainbow Fair is more than that now because my friends and I made it into something that mattered to us.

"And maybe we gave up too much of our own community because of fear and silence," Dad says softly. "The community you've created here reminds us of what we've lost."

Tears clog my throat as I think of Mom touching the Demirs' prayer rug and Dad touching the dusty cover of the English Quran and telling me that it was mine.

"This can be your community too," I say. "There's a local mosque Anna took me to. Maybe we can go there sometime."

Mom looks startled. "You went to a mosque?"

I bite my lip. "Yeah. They were having a community barbecue, and Anna took me. I'm sorry I went without telling you and didn't talk about Anna either, but she's awesome and so is her family."

Mom smiles. "I can see that."

"Yes." Dad nods. "I think I'd like to go to that mosque with you sometime."

My parents gather me into their arms, and right there, in the middle of a smelly gym littered with deflated rainbow balloons and glitter, I feel right at home at the strangest and best Rainbow Fair ever.

I still have a lot of questions. Like—will my family reconnect with our faith? How are my friendships going to change even more? And . . . what kind of Chinese Muslim am I going to be?

I don't know the answers to any of these questions, but I *do* know one thing.

I'll be the one to decide who I am.

Twenty-Five

"Where are we going again?" I ask as we walk into the mall.

"It's a surprise," Katie replies, and I remember my mom saying something just like that before she took me to buy a qípáo. I'm pretty sure Katie isn't taking me to buy traditional Chinese dresses this time.

Megan, Allie, and Shane exchange knowing glances, but Anna looks just as puzzled as I am. Before, it would have felt like Anna and I were being left out of some group secret, but everything is different after yesterday's Rainbow Fair. We all understand each other better now, so I don't assume we're being excluded, but I still wonder what the surprise is.

"Is it a new store?" Anna asks.

"Not exactly," Shane says, "but I think you'll like it."

Hmm. So it's a surprise for us. "Is it something Anna and I will like or something all of us will like?"

Megan's eyes sparkle. "We'll all like it, but mostly you and Anna."

"No more questions!" Allie's tone is a bit bossy, but I don't mind. It's just how she is when she wants things to go perfectly, and I'm touched that she's so invested.

Despite Allie's declaration of no more questions, Anna and I keep making guesses as we walk down the length of the mall.

"Mall bumper cars?" Anna asks.

Megan laughs. "Is that even a thing?"

"It should be a thing," Shane says, "but no, there are no bumper cars here."

We pass a bookstore, and excitement shivers through me. I think I know what our surprise is. "It's a book reading by one of the authors we had on display at Rainbow Fair!"

"No, but that's a good guess," Katie says.

Darn. I thought I had figured it out. "Am I on the right track?"

"Not even close," Allie says smugly. Apparently, she's decided that forbidding questions is a lost cause.

"How about a hint?" I ask.

Shane shakes their head. "We're almost there. You don't have to wait long."

Katie stops. "Allie and Megan, can you two get the items?"

Items. That's not weirdly mysterious or ominous at all.

"On it," Megan says, and she and Allie take off.

Katie whips out two thin scarves from her backpack. "Okay,

we really want this to be a surprise, so do you mind wearing blindfolds?"

I couldn't have heard her right. "Wait. What?"

Anna is already reaching for one. "Ooh. How fun!" Is there nothing that girl isn't enthusiastic about?

Katie shoots me a grin. "Anna's on board. Come on, Sophie. Where's your sense of adventure?"

"You do know we're teens at a mall and not spies caught breaking into a military compound and that those are just scarves from your mom's closet," I mutter, but I take the scarf anyway because I'm starting to get caught up in everyone's excitement.

Katie ties the scarf around my head, covering my eyes, and I'm assuming Shane is doing the same for Anna.

"Is that too tight?" Shane asks.

"It's perfect," Anna says cheerfully.

"Can you see anything?" Katie tugs at the ends of the knotted scarf.

"No." I can actually still sort of see through the gauzy fabric of the scarf, but not enough to make out anything but vague shapes.

"Okay, let's go." Katie takes me by the hand and leads me forward.

I know she's not going to let me run into a wall and I can see enough to avoid obstacles, so I let her lead me.

We make our way forward slowly because of the blindfolds. I'm sure people are staring at us, but it doesn't bother me as much as I thought it would. Katie is right. This does feel like an adventure.

We walk for a few minutes before Katie says, "We're here!"

That's weird. We didn't seem to enter a store or anything. In fact, I can see enough to make me think we're just in the food court. I reach for the scarf, but she adds, "Keep your blindfold on."

I roll my eyes before I remember my eyes are covered.

"This is so much fun," Anna says.

"There's a chair in front of you," Shane says to Anna, "and I'm going to help you sit, but be careful and go slowly."

Katie grips my elbow. "There's a chair for you too, Sophie." She guides me into my seat, which feels hard and plastic.

Yeah, this is definitely the food court.

Before I can ask what we're doing here, footsteps approach. "We're back!" Allie's voice sounds breathless like she's been hurrying.

"And we have the items," Megan says, also breathless.

There's a clattering sound of trays being set on the table.

The smell hits my nose, and automatically, I try to place it. It's rich and pungent and strangely both different and familiar.

If I didn't know better, I'd think it was hot dogs. Surely our friends aren't expecting us to eat pork?

"What does your magic nose tell you, Sophie?" Katie asks eagerly.

"Um . . ." I literally don't know what to say.

"Let them take off the blindfolds," Shane says.

"Yeah." Megan sounds sympathetic. "Don't make them keep guessing."

"I want them to see this," Allie adds.

I'm not so sure I agree. Do I want to see this? Well, it's not like I can stay blindfolded forever.

I take off the scarf, and instantly, my gaze locks on the fat hot dogs in white paper cartons. *Oh no.* I thought that's what I was smelling. My heart sinks.

Anna is also staring at the hot dogs. "This is nice of you to treat us to lunch, but Muslims don't eat pork."

"Of course," Allie replies.

"That's why this is perfect," Megan adds.

"When Katie told us you can never eat the hot dogs at school, we knew we had to bring you here," Shane says.

My head is spinning. "I don't understand."

"Vegan hot dogs!" Katie says triumphantly. "This place just added them to their menu."

"Separate grill and everything," Shane assures us. "We

checked, and the vegan hot dogs don't come into contact with the pork ones."

"Katie said you like your burgers with ketchup, mustard, and relish, so that's what we got for you, Sophie." Megan points to the hot dog in front of me, slathered with my favorite condiments.

"We didn't know what you wanted on yours, Anna." Allie places a bunch of condiment packages on the table. "So we got you these."

Anna claps her hands together. "Vegan hot dogs? That's amazing."

It is. For no reason at all, my eyes fill with water. I can't believe they did this for us.

"Sophie?" Katie peers at me anxiously. "Are you okay?"

I sniffle. "Better than okay." I pick up my hot dog and look around at all my friends. At the start of the Rainbow Fair preparation, I had exactly one friend . . . and I felt I was losing her.

I thought we had to be completely alike to be friends, but that's not true. Rainbow Fair taught me that all the ways we're different can bring us closer together. Katie and I are stronger than ever now, and I have all these new friends too.

Even though I've only known Anna for a month, I can't imagine my life without her. She makes everything twice as fun when I get to do it with her. And then there's Shane, Megan, and Allie, who care enough to take us to get vegan hot dogs and make it into an adventure.

I take a bite of my vegan hot dog, and the tanginess of the condiments with the slight smokiness of the hot dog is perfect. It tastes like everything I've ever wanted.

"This," I say, my heart full of gratitude, "is the best surprise ever." My words don't seem like quite enough, and I wish there was a way to say how important this moment is.

"Hamdullah," Anna says, smiling at me, and this feels as much of a gift as the hot dog from the others. "That's short for 'Alhamdulillah,' which means 'all praise to Allah.'"

Yes. That's what I feel. So thankful that I want to shout it to the heavens. Something shifts inside me that I can't quite explain. I take a deep breath. Even though I won't be able to say it perfectly, maybe it doesn't matter. This word of my faith will be true to what is in my heart.

"Alhamdulillah."

Acknowledgments

I have so many people to thank for this book. First and foremost, I want to thank everyone involved with the Muslim Storytellers Fellowship through the Highlights Foundation and sponsored by the Doris Duke Foundation. As I said in my dedication, this story would not have been possible without you.

I can't say enough about how much my cohort in the Muslim Storytellers Fellowship means to me. Ashley Franklin, Autumn Allen, Aya Khalil, Farhiya Samatar, Fatima Samatar, Haneen Oriqat, Heba Helmy, Huda Al-Marashi, Intisar Khanani, Khadijah VanBrakle, Loretta Chefchaouni, Melinda González, Mustaali Raj, Natasha Khan Kazi, Rhonda Roumani, and Selime Okuyan—you are all incredible storytellers, and more than that, you are my family.

Thank you to all the programming committee members and the mentors for the Muslim Storytellers Fellowship—Hatem Aly, Hena Khan, Jamilah Thompkins-Bigelow, M. O. Yuksel, Nafiza Azad, Narmeen Lakhani, S. A. Chakraborty,

S. K. Ali, Sabaa Tahir, and Zaynah Qutubuddin. I hope you know what a beautiful community you have created.

My book ends with this passage, and this is also how I feel about my Muslim Storytellers family:

Yes. That's what I feel. So thankful that I want to shout it to the heavens. Something shifts inside me that I can't quite explain. I take a deep breath. Even though I won't be able to say it perfectly, maybe it doesn't matter. This word of my faith will be true to what is in my heart.

"Alhamdulillah."

Thank you to everyone at the Highlights Foundation, especially Alison Green Myers and Alexandra Villasante, and George Brown. Alison and Alex, you have been my much-needed guides in so many ways (and yes, I mean that literally too).

I also have so much gratitude to everyone at Clarion Books. Multiple wonderful editors were involved in this book. My deepest thanks go out to Angela Song, who first asked me to pitch her a middle grade contemporary book about a Hui protagonist. I was also fortunate to have the incredible Alessandra Preziosi and Erica Wainer as editors. You both edited my book with such lovely nuance and insight, and I am so grateful for the care you took with *Rainbow Fair*. I first pitched this story as "intersectionality for middle graders," and I'm grateful for the enthusiastic response everyone had for that pitch! Thank you to everyone in design, editing, and marketing as well. You are all incredible!

No acknowledgments would be complete without my heartfelt thanks to my wonderful agents, Christa Heschke and Daniele Hunter. You both gave me so much encouragement and support when I first shared my pitch with you.

Of course, I want to thank my absolutely incredible beta readers.

Loretta Chefchaouni, I am so grateful for the insight you brought to my story and your excellent, generous feedback. This book became so much richer and fuller thanks to your suggestions. Thank you, my dear friend.

Tanisha Brandon-Felder, your dedication to young readers and equity is truly an inspiration, and your thoughtful feedback meant everything to this book. Thank you for your beautiful insights on my characters and their world.

Thank you also to Christina Scheuer, my constant and brilliant feedback partner and friend. You were invaluable as I talked through difficult scenes and tried to make sense of what it was I was trying to do! Thank you to Narmeen Lakhani for your beautiful facilitation of an incredibly helpful workshop at one of the Muslim Storytellers Fellowship retreats at Highlights.

As always, thank you to my parents, my husband, and my

children. Mom and Dad, my deepest thanks for the constant refrain of "By the way, you're still Muslim." Joel, thank you for encouraging me to apply for the Muslim Storytellers Fellowship. Liam and Kieran, thank you for being exactly who you are, whoever that may be. I love you and will always fight for you.

Thank you so much to YOU, my dear readers!

I'd like to end by saying that I was doing my final edits at the end of 2023. Needless to say, it was hard to be writing a positive and joyful story about a girl exploring her Muslim identity during an increase of anti-Muslim hate. And, of course, my heart was breaking and is still breaking for the Palestinian people.

Yet, I continued to write through my grief because I believe that stories are necessary and humanizing in what can be a dehumanizing world.

My book is about middle schoolers coming together to celebrate multifaceted diverse cultures in their own way. I hope my story about Sophie and her friends learning to understand each other is a humanizing one.